SOFTER THAN VELVET, STRONGER THAN STEEL

WAYNE DRAYER

Inspiring Voices®
A Service of Guideposts

Inspiring Voices books may be ordered through booksellers or by contacting:

Inspiring Voices
1663 Liberty Drive
Bloomington, IN 47403
www.inspiringvoices.com
1 (866) 697-5313

ISBN: 978-1-4624-0809-2 (sc)
ISBN: 978-1-4624-0810-8 (e)

Library of Congress Control Number: 2013919560

Printed in the United States of America.

Inspiring Voices rev. date: 11/21/2013

Contents

ACKNOWLEDGMENTS

O beautiful, for spacious skies,
For amber waves of grain;

It would be incomplete to publish this book
without acknowledging many contributors.

Above all, gratitude goes to God, the author of liberty.
In Proverbs 3:6, we are encouraged with: "In all thy ways
acknowledge him, and he shall direct thy paths."

All scripture references are from the King
James Version of the Bible.

The rich history of the United States is drawn from credible
resources, including encyclopedias, history textbooks, Internet
sites, the US Constitution, and the Northwest Ordinance.

The town of Bridges is symbolic, part of
the storyline, not an actual place.

Selections from "In the Garden" and "The Battle
Hymn of the Republic" were written by C. Austin
Miles and Julia Ward Howe, respectively.

Finally, family, personal acquaintances, and fellow travelers
throughout life have offered invaluable insight. The personalities
of many of these combined to contribute to the composite
of characters in the storyline. As the golden grains of wheat
and corn are shielded by the husk and stalk until delivered
to the harvest, so the enduring truths of the historical
fiction novel are carried and delivered by the storyline.

Part One

We have staked the whole future of our new nation, not upon the power of government; far from it. We have staked the future of all our political constitutions upon the capacity of each of ourselves to govern ourselves according to the moral principles of the Ten Commandments.
—James Madison, "Father of the Constitution," fourth president of the United States

Train up a child in the way he should go: and when he is old, he will not depart from it.
—Proverbs 22:6

So great is my veneration for the Bible that the earlier my children begin to read it the more confident will be my hope that they will prove useful citizens of their country and respectable members of society.
—John Quincy Adams, sixth president of the United States

FAMILY FOUNDATIONS

A. J. huddled with some of his classmates beneath the canopy of Bridges Junior High School as they waited for their parents to arrive. Darkness, coupled with cold, drizzling rain, reduced the visibility offered by dim streetlights. The rain did not bother him. Tyler Renken's remarks did.

"I should have gotten the lead part," Tyler grumbled to a friend, "not A. J."

The friend remained silent and nervously glanced in A. J.'s direction. Tyler continued, unaware how his voice carried.

"The only reason he won the part was because his mom always makes costumes for the play. Every year, it's the same old story. It's time for her to cool it."

Quietness enveloped the group when A. J. confronted Tyler.

"Hey, Tyler, if you have something to say, say it to me. You can rag on me all you want, but don't criticize my mother."

"I wasn't being critical. I was just—"

"Stop! I don't even want to hear it!"

A. J. saw his mother's blue Chevy pulling up across the street. With one long look of disgust toward his classmate, he turned and splashed his way to the car.

"Mom, you've been crying!" A. J. exclaimed. He quickly closed the car door. "What happened?"

Loretta Franklin put the car in drive and slowly edged out of the circular driveway onto Mill Creek Road leading out of town.

"You don't look so happy yourself, son. What's troubling you? Didn't the tryouts go well?"

"That went okay, but that's part of the problem."

"What do you mean?" she asked.

"Mr. Harnel gave me the lead part. Then Tyler was complaining to others that he should have gotten it."

"Oh, things like that happen, A. J. Some people always try to blame others when things don't go their way. You just have to shrug it off."

"I know. That really didn't bother me. It was what he said next that got me."

"What was that?"

"He dragged you into it."

"Me?"

"Yeah. He said the only reason I got the part was because you make the costumes every year—and he didn't say it very nice! That upset me. We argued. I'm glad you came when you did."

"You don't need to worry about that hurting my feelings."

"But I do! You didn't do anything to hurt anyone. Besides, I thought Tyler and I were good friends."

"You always have been, A. J."

"We probably won't be after today."

"Oh, I think you will. True friendship doesn't shatter easily. Just give it time," his mother replied.

A. J. studied the rhythmic motion of the windshield wipers as they deflected the rain.

"Do you think he's right, Mom?"

"About what?"

"About that being the only reason I won the part."

"Oh, no," Loretta said, laughing. "I know Mr. Harnel very well. He would not have given you the lead part unless he definitely thought you deserved it. He demands the very best."

His mother placed her right hand on A. J.'s arm. Her soft voice penetrated his heart.

"Aaron, I'm not surprised you got the lead part."

"You're not?"

"No. I've known for a long time you have a special gift."

"Really?"

"Yes. It's obvious to me."

"Mom, it's been a long time since you called me Aaron."

"It just seemed like the right thing to say."

A. J. felt speechless. *Why is it that she can make my problems appear like nothing?* he thought. *This is just like when she used to hold me and whisper words like* Aaron, miracle, *and* special.

"Well," he said suddenly, "that's enough of me! You've been troubled too. Why have you been crying?"

"Oh, it's been a terrible day, A. J. I'm sure you've heard about our nation's tragedy."

"Oh, yeah! Everyone at school was shook up. I'm glad we had the real tryouts last night. This evening we just read through the play together. I don't think I could have done a good job tonight after hearing that news."

Loretta turned on the radio in time for the nine o'clock evening news.

"The nation was stunned and saddened today by a shooting in Dallas, Texas. President John Kennedy was struck by an assassin's bullet while traveling in a motorcade through this beautiful city. A suspect is in custody, a family is in shock, and a grieving nation is in turmoil," the newscaster reported in a sad, sober voice.

Loretta turned the radio off.

"Do you remember when he became president, A. J.?"

"About all I remember is seeing a man who looked like he had a lot of energy."

"He was energetic, A. J. He had a heart for our country. It's hard to believe something like this could happen in America."

"It's like a bad fairy tale, Mom!"

5

"I weep for our country, A. J. We have been so blessed in America, yet so many don't seem to recognize it!"

She reached for another tissue to dry her eyes and then looked at her son and smiled.

"Let's talk about something more pleasant until we get home."

"Okay. How are plans for the big weekend shaping up?" A. J. asked happily.

"Things seem to be coming along fairly well. I've still got more food to prepare. Dad is at the high school now helping set up."

"Mom," A. J. interrupted, "this celebration is in honor of all the veterans, right?"

"That's right."

"Well, then, I was wondering, why do we have it near the end of November instead of the weekend of Veterans Day?" A. J. asked.

"You know, we used to have it on that weekend. Then one year it didn't work out to have it on that date, so we postponed it till later in the month. And you know what?"

"What?"

"Almost everyone seemed to like it better. More people were home. Things weren't so busy. I think the extra time in between seems to tie the calendar Veterans Day to our Veterans Day celebration. It has become the big annual event in Bridges, especially since we've added a high school senior to give a speech," his mother explained.

"That was a good addition," A. J. added. "I like it."

"Wait till you see Jessie, A. J. She is really excited about giving her speech."

"She is so cool, Mom. I can't wait to hear it. What's it going to be about?"

"It will be a little different from speeches in the past. She's going to involve a person from our county whose great-grandfather fought during the Civil War."

"Wow! That's dynamite! This could be one of the best celebrations we've ever had. I'm surprised no one thought of doing that before. I'm glad Jessie is the one who gets to do it, aren't you?"

"Oh, for sure," Mrs. Franklin replied. "I know she's ready. It should be a super weekend. I'm afraid, though, that the assassination could put a damper on everything."

"Maybe it will give the whole weekend more meaning," A. J. offered. "After all, it is our Veterans Day celebration."

"You know, son, you could be right. I never thought of it like that. Jessie's topic could fit very nicely with what happened today. Maybe future senior class speakers will follow her lead."

"In what way, Mom?"

"We should focus more on how and why our country was founded, before we forget and risk losing it. Liberty is our trademark. Our young president who left us today often defended …" Loretta's voice quavered. "A. J., is the rain playing tricks or is that car swerving into—"

A. J. felt the sudden jolt and heard the screeching sound of metal against metal before the blue Chevy left the roadway in a tumbling free fall and plummeted toward the ravine floor thirty feet below. Screams pierced the air—whether his or his mother's, he couldn't tell. Branches snapped and vegetation was ripped from the ravine walls as the vehicle fell; then there was the final thud of the car colliding with the ground.

The spinning stopped. Quietness settled like a blanket. He felt his mother's body draped over him. For a few glorious moments, he imagined being home in bed and his mother waking him. All too soon, reality clawed its way back into his consciousness. He moaned weakly.

"Mom?"

No answer.

Trembling with fear, he tried again.

"Mom?"

Then … blackness.

7

The minister spoke directly to the family sitting in the front pew. "You can't see all the people behind you. The assembly room is filled. There are many people also sitting in the fellowship area beyond this room."

He paused a few moments before continuing.

"I know this may not mean a lot to you right now. But in the coming days, you can remember how people came to support you today."

A timid smile creased Joseph's face. The comforting words did very little to fill the vacant spot in his heart once occupied by his soul mate.

Beside him sat Jessie, his seventeen-year-old daughter. She had been excited about attending a small Christian college in Tennessee after graduating from high school the following spring. Suddenly, the glow of those plans faded like embers preparing to turn to ash.

A. J. sat beside his sister. His left arm was supported by a sling, and his face was hidden from view. Part of him remained in the ravine.

The fourth person with the family was Loretta's mother, affectionately known by many as Grandma Wilken. Loretta's legacy belonged to this lovely woman. They were alike in many ways. She was thirty years older than Loretta. Never had it occurred to her that she would one day attend her youngest daughter's funeral.

Turning his attention to the congregation, the minister's words came slowly but clearly.

"We have lost someone very dear to each of us. Loretta possessed that rare combination of talent, generosity, and genuine humility. It is difficult to see her go."

Doc Roberts, a close friend, sat behind the family. Nearly at retirement age, he still kept in close touch with the Franklins.

The Wilken family had befriended Doc when he first moved to Bridges, West Virginia, in 1930. He needed time to establish a practice. The caring couple took him in. Their instant friendship had never lost the flames of appreciation.

After the opening comments, Doc Roberts found it difficult to concentrate on the sermon. His mind was drifting back over the years, recreating many experiences shared with the family. The scenes flashed by, settling at last on a pivotal event. He could picture the room clearly, and although it was a hospital room, it was awash with happiness—the day Loretta's nightmare had come to an end.

Loretta's soft voice had kept the doctor from leaving the hospital room that morning. He had just turned and spoken in a gentle tone to the young woman holding her newborn.

"Congratulations, Mrs. Franklin. Your miracle child has safely arrived. I'll leave you and Joe alone a few minutes."

"Oh, please don't go, Doctor," she had whispered in a barely audible voice. "You've been through so much with us. We'd like you to enjoy this moment too."

Her husband nodded and smiled. The doctor found a comfortable chair and joined the circle of happiness.

Several minutes passed while Joe and Loretta gazed lovingly at their son. Only their occasional sniffs and wiping of tears broke the tender silence. The shafts of sunlight through the window seemed to herald a new era of hope for them.

"I remember so clearly, Loretta, the day your mother held you like you are holding your son. She is a treasure, so peaceful and kind. You remind me of her."

"Oh, thank you, Doctor. You couldn't give me a better compliment."

She looked down at her baby again and then back to her husband. "Did you call Mother, Joe?"

"Yes, I did. She and Jessie should be here in just a few minutes."

More silence followed while they allowed the wonder of the moment to fill their hearts. Without looking up, Loretta broke the stillness.

"It's been a long road, Doc. We're so grateful to you for sticking with us."

"I really don't know what to say," Doc murmured. "I would have done whatever I could for your happiness. But, of course, a doctor's power can go only so far."

"Five years into our marriage, we began to wonder if we would have any children at all. And then we were given our lovely daughter, Jessie. We were so grateful." Loretta paused before continuing. "But we wanted at least one more child."

"I knew you did," Doc responded. "I could see the extreme disappointment in your eyes after the first miscarriage."

Loretta looked at Joseph and Doc. "I don't know what I would have done without the steadying influence of both of you, especially after the second and third miscarriages. It was awful."

Joseph dried the tears on his wife's face with a tissue. "Those days are gone. Let's concentrate on what we have now."

Doc Roberts remained silent. He recalled his conversation with Loretta's mother a year after the third miscarriage, when Loretta was again carrying a child.

"I'm concerned about your daughter's health," he had told her. "I don't know if she will be able to deliver this child, but I'll do what I can to help. Be sure I am notified immediately if anything abnormal begins to happen."

Two emergency trips to the hospital during that nine-month period caused old fears to resurface. The couple expected the same bitter result. But both times, Doc Roberts was able to stabilize the situation, and their hopes rebounded.

"Last night, I was frightened when the pains started coming closer together," Loretta said with tears starting down her face again. "Thank God you were home when we called."

"I'll admit, I was a bit anxious myself."

"You know, Doc, Joe and I have been so tentative throughout this pregnancy—we wouldn't even allow ourselves to talk about a name for the baby. Do you think that's unnatural?"

"After everything you two have been through," the doctor reassured, "I don't think that's unnatural at all."

Turning to her husband, she asked, "Have you thought of a name, Joe?"

"You're much better at that than I am, Loretta. Besides, I think the name for our daughter was kind of my idea in the beginning. Your expression tells me you have a name in mind."

"You know me too well." Loretta laughed. "Since I saw it was a boy, one name keeps coming to my mind. I really don't know why, but it does."

All eyes remained on the child. Then, like butterflies dancing on the summer breeze, Loretta's soft voice enhanced the sacred moment.

"Honey, let's name him Aaron."

Joe's strong hand gently squeezed his wife's shoulder. Keeping his gaze fixed on his son, he silently nodded his agreement.

With the peacefulness of a ship gliding into the harbor, Loretta softly echoed her thoughts.

"Aaron Joseph—our miracle child."

"The Lord is my shepherd; I shall not want. He maketh me to lie down in green pastures: he leadeth me beside the still waters. He restoreth my soul: he leadeth me in the paths of righteousness for his name's sake. Yea, though I walk through the valley of the shadow of death, I will fear no evil: for thou art with me; thy rod and thy staff they comfort me. Thou preparest a table before me in the presence of mine enemies: thou annointest my head with oil; my cup runneth over. Surely goodness and mercy shall follow me all the days of my life: and I will dwell in the house of the Lord for ever."

Although he had heard this psalm spoken many times before, this time Doc Roberts felt a stinging in his eyes. He focused as the minister concluded his message.

"We will now accompany the family to Loretta's final resting place," the pastor intoned before stepping down from the pulpit.

Everyone, except a few who had difficulty walking, followed the family and the pallbearers who carried the casket up a small rise to the cemetery behind the church. The crisp air complemented the pleasant sunshine, almost as a tribute to the beloved person being mourned by a community. When everyone was gathered, the minister spoke again.

"We will begin this final service by listening to the choir sing one of Loretta's favorites, 'In the Garden.'"

Many wept while others tried to join in singing.

> I come to the garden alone, while the dew is still on
> the roses;
> And the voice I hear falling on my ear, the Son of
> God discloses;
> And He walks with me and He talks with me,
> And He tells me I am His own;
> And the joy we share while we tarry there,
> None other has ever known.

The remaining two verses allowed time for tender reflection. When the singing stopped, the minister added a few comments.

"Flowers and gardens were precious to Loretta. It just comes to me now that, before our final prayer, each of us, in the privacy of thought, can ponder how Loretta helped our lives blossom."

Then, for the first time anyone could remember, a strange but stirring thing happened. The ponderings of the hearts metamorphosed into words, dropping among the group like leaves drifting from trees in the autumn air. It began with one of Loretta's neighbors. Despite her emotion, she communicated her thoughts with a broken voice.

"I feel so lost right now. There has never been anyone so willing to take time to listen—no matter how busy she was. She helped me so much. I will miss her dearly."

The mayor seized upon the moment. "We can ill afford to lose someone of Loretta's caliber. I'll miss her enthusiasm and talents."

"She helped us every year at the school, even before she had children there," the principal added.

"We all love our children," a young mother softly joined in, "but her devotion to her family was special. I'll miss her example."

Ten or fifteen people voiced their thoughts. Others wanted to but couldn't find the words or the voice to do so. When it seemed the comments were exhausted, the minister spoke the closing prayer. For several minutes, everyone remained in place and silently grieved once more with the family. Then, slowly, they made their way back down the incline to the church.

TROUBLED WATERS

T wo months elapsed before Doc Roberts received a call
from his close friend, Judge Evans. He wanted to arrange
a casual get-together with Grandma Wilken. Doc made
the arrangements to meet at the Across the Square restaurant the
following Tuesday.

From his upstairs chambers, Judge Evans watched Doc and
Grandma approach the diner. After a few moments had passed, he
crossed the square to join them. Inside the well-lit gathering place,
they were led to a quiet cubicle in the back room.

Introductions were not necessary. The three had been
instrumental in joining efforts to launch several successful programs
in the community. But this meeting was not to talk about another
program. After the usual informal conversation, Judge Evans came
right to the point.

"I've been burdened ever since the terrible tragedy in our
community. I wanted to allow enough time to pass so that we could
talk rationally, but not too much time that our senses would be dulled.
Is my timing okay, Grandma?"

"Yes—yes, I think so. It's been a tough time, but, yes, I think we
can talk."

"Good. I'm glad you are here, Doc. Your involvement with this
family speaks for itself in many positive ways."

"Thank you, Judge. I've been burdened also, and I'm happy for this chance to talk."

"I can't imagine, Grandma, what it is to lose a child. I know you are no stranger to losing loved ones, but that certainly doesn't make it any easier to face this."

"Nothing could prepare a person for this," she responded. "Watching this beautiful family try to cope makes it all the more difficult."

"That leads directly to my next question." The judge took another swallow of coffee and then carefully cleared his throat. "How are the youngsters doing?"

"It's a struggle," Grandma said softly, while gazing out the window. "Actually, Jessie seems to be coping fairly well. Of course, she's older."

"And she wasn't directly involved in the accident like A. J. was," Doc Roberts interjected.

"Yes, that's true," Grandma replied. "But still, the boy seems so different. I'm really worried."

An uneasy silence boxed their conversation. Judge Evans, at length, spoke up again.

"That's what I was afraid of. I'm especially concerned about the boy. Oh, I'm concerned about Jessie too. I hope she doesn't trash her plans about continuing her education after graduation. She has a lot to offer."

"With time, I think Jessie will be okay," Grandma responded. "At first, she wanted to do just what you feared and forget about going on. But now she's warming up to the idea again. She's already been accepted at a Christian college in Tennessee, you know."

"Good," replied the judge. "That's a relief. A. J., however, seems to be a different story. I hardly know the boy, but when I saw that vacant look in his eyes, one of the rare times he made eye contact …" Shaking his head, he continued. "In my position, I've seen too many people headed for trouble who had that vacant stare. He's going to need a lot of help."

With difficulty, Grandma tried to organize her thoughts.

"No one can get close to him. He's just kind of withdrawing into himself. Sometimes he talks a little with Jessie, but he is very guarded about what he says," she explained.

"I'm not surprised," Doc Roberts offered. "He and his mother were very close. The difficulty surrounding Loretta's pregnancy and A. J.'s birth naturally produced an unusually close bond. I've never seen such a special mother-son relationship. Now, not only has A. J. lost his mother—he also lost his best friend."

"That does help explain some of it," the judge agreed. "But, Grandma, do you think he is holding a lot of resentment against the driver of the other car and just not able or willing to express it?"

"Well, somewhat, of course." Grandma was careful with her words. "But it's even worse than that."

"Worse than that?" Judge Evans echoed Doc's thoughts also. "What do you mean?"

Grandma stirred her coffee very slowly before answering. Meeting the puzzled gazes of the gentlemen, she replied, "I think he's also blaming himself. I think he's shouldering too much of the load. I think he's convinced that he is the cause—of his mother's death."

"Jess?"

The inflection of A. J.'s voice caused her to look up from her reading. It sounded like old times when he used to come into her room to ask an important question. She had missed that the last couple of months, so she was more than willing to give her full attention.

"Yes?" she responded in a quiet voice.

"Can we talk for a while?" he asked.

"Sure! Come in. Close the door if you'd like."

A. J. walked in slowly and quietly closed the door behind him. He found a rocking chair close to Jessie and sat down. He seemed nervous to her at first, but he soon relaxed before speaking again.

"I was just wondering how you are doing."

"It's difficult, A. J., very difficult. Sometimes I just want to talk to her so badly, but I know I can't. I just keep trying to learn to accept it."

A. J. stared at the floor a bit before lifting his eyes with the next question.

"Do you remember that short service for Mom at the cemetery, Jess?"

"Yes," she answered. "I think everyone was taken by surprise!"

"Well, all those nice things they said about Mom—do you think they were true?"

"Of course they were true. I don't think anyone was making things up."

"I agree," said A. J. "Mom was a wonderful person, wasn't she?"

"Well, A. J., no one is perfect. Mom had her faults like everyone else. But in all the years I've lived, and all the people I've come in contact with, she was as close to perfect as anyone I've known."

"I feel that way too. So let me ask you a question."

Jessie braced herself.

"If Mom was that kind, and talented, and helpful, and needed by so many people, why did she have to go?"

"That is a very tough question, A. J. I've thought about the same thing myself. After thinking about it and thinking about it, this is what I've come up with."

A. J. leaned forward in the chair, as though he was waiting to learn the mysteries of the universe.

"I've come to the conclusion that God has reasons for everything that happens. He has something for people to learn through all of this. We may not know what it is now, but sometime we will discover the reason."

A. J. slumped back in his chair with a clear look of disappointment on his face.

"No, Jessie, I can't accept that!"

"Why not?"

"Listen," A. J. said intently. "We say God is good, right?"

"Yes, that's correct."

"Okay. If God is good, then He wants people with good qualities to spread that goodness for Him, right?"

Jessie nodded her head slightly, although she knew where A. J. was going with his argument.

"So Mom was the perfect—what would we say—representative for God here on earth. She could show His goodness to other people better than anyone else around here. Why, then, would God take her away when she was doing such a great job?"

"Well, A. J., it's difficult to understand the reason now. Maybe we won't understand it for quite a while."

"No, sister, I can't accept that. How can Mom be taken away from us when you and I need her so badly? When so many people need her so badly?"

"I wish I could give you a suitable answer, A. J. We don't understand right now. Perhaps as we grow older, we will see the reason more clearly."

A. J. suddenly stopped talking and sat silently for nearly a minute. Jessie was afraid she had pushed him back into himself again. Soon, however, he looked up calmly and locked Jessie's gaze with his eyes. He spoke softly but with conviction that caused Jessie to feel a chill.

"I know the reason."

"You do?" Jessie said while leaning forward. After a slight hesitation, she asked, "What is it?"

"Me."

"You?" Jessie said incredulously. "What do you mean?"

"Well, look at the facts, Jessie. I was the reason Mom left home that night to go to the school. I was the reason she was driving that car in the rain on that dark evening when another car hit us. I was the reason! If not for me, she would have been safe at home that night."

"A. J.! You must never allow yourself to think like that! That accident was not your fault!"

"And I was the reason you didn't get to give that speech you had worked so hard to prepare because everything was changed that weekend. You can blame me."

"A. J., that is not true!"

A worried smile creased A. J.'s lips as he looked deeply into Jessie's eyes. She tried to find the trusting little brother she had always known. But what she saw was a confused adolescent, pleading for help but not knowing how to find it.

A. J. slowly picked himself up out of the chair and walked out of the room. He gently pulled the door closed behind him.

Christmas for Grandma Wilken and the Franklins had been the emptiest they had ever known. Easter sunrise service lost some of its luster for them that year, and the Fourth of July was just another day.

Joe continued his assistant plant manager duties at a glass factory in a nearby town. Jessie used the summer to make final preparations to enter the Christian college in Tennessee. Grandma tried to become more involved with the local volunteer groups to keep her mind off of her daughter. And A. J. continued to mystify everyone.

"A. J., I'm going to miss you this fall when I go away to school," Jessie told him about a month before summer ended.

"So why are you going then?" he asked with little emotion.

"I really mean it, A. J. Look, I'm still your sister, and you're still my brother. I want you to be happy like you were last year and all the years before that. It will make me sad knowing you are back here in Bridges not enjoying life. I know it's difficult, but we've got to at least try."

A. J. said nothing. He just kept staring at the table.

"Two of your teachers talked to me this summer, A. J. They are frustrated about what is happening. Your grades have fallen two levels from the As and Bs you always were getting."

A. J. shrugged and said, "I'm still passing. What's the big deal?"

"Look, A. J. You're going to be a freshman this year. Things are going to get tougher. If you fall too far behind, you will have a hard time catching up. Four years will go by pretty fast, and then you'll have bigger decisions to make."

"Four years won't go by quick enough to suit me."

"Try to get involved with something, A. J. Coach told me he couldn't wait for you to get to high school. He watched you play when you were younger, and he said you had special talents in just about any sport. He really wants you to play. He knows you can help the team."

"He's got plenty of others he can use. Why would I want to get involved?"

"I can't believe you really mean what you are saying, A. J. You never were like this before, and you know Mom wouldn't—"

"Mom wouldn't what?" he asked forcefully.

"Well, Mom wouldn't want you to waste your talents and abilities; you know that."

"But Mom's not here, is she? That makes all the difference."

Jessie cradled her head in her arms and wept openly. To her surprise, A. J. came across the room and gently rubbed her shoulders. After a few minutes, she looked up at his expressionless face. With tear-filled eyes, she softly implored, "Please try while I'm gone, A. J. Please try."

ALONE

A. J. remained unapproachable. He did enough to get by in school. He lived with his father, Joe, but there was minimal father-son interaction. There was no animosity, but each of them nurtured their own dreams or nightmares of the past. Grandma tried to enter his domain with coaching from Doc Roberts and Judge Evans. She met with very little success. A. J. occasionally exchanged letters with Jessie, keeping their relationship civil.

Mainly, A. J. spent his time stocking shelves at the local grocery store. Three years had passed, and the continual physical exercise was evident in the rippling muscles filling out his six-foot, one-inch frame. The news today, however, was not good for A. J. when he finished working. His boss had come to him after lunch.

"I need to talk with you a minute before you leave today, A. J."

Mr. Bowden, the store owner, never spoke much, so A. J. was rather concerned as quitting time approached.

"You wanted to talk to me, Mr. Bowden? It's about four o'clock, so I'll soon be clocking out."

"Yes, I did, A. J. Thanks for reminding me."

Mr. Bowden pulled up a chair and offered one for A. J. to sit on.

"A. J., you know you have been one of my best employees the last couple of years. You've done your job well, and I have no complaints."

"I appreciate working here, sir."

21

Mr. Bowden smiled, but he quickly turned sober again.

"My two grandsons from Kansas are coming to spend the summer with me. They're going to be here in about two weeks."

"Are they the sons of your daughter who is ill?" A. J. asked.

"Yes. You remember us talking about that?"

"Yes, I do."

"Well," Mr. Bowden continued, "her condition is getting worse. She won't be able to take care of the boys this summer, so they are coming to live with us. My problem is, well, they need a job. You know how hard it is to find work, especially for newcomers."

"So you need to give them a job here at the store, is that right?" A. J. asked.

"I'm sorry, A. J. That's correct. I'm going to have to let a couple of you boys go for the summer. But I'd like to have you come back next fall. Could you do that?"

"I guess it depends on what happens this summer, but I'd like to."

"I regret that this has to happen, A. J. If any of these plans change, I'll let you know. Thanks for understanding. I hope you have a good summer."

The sun beat down as A. J. trudged along the dusty gravel road leading to the valley. Another day, another disappointment, another thing to weigh him down. The more he thought about it, the more his mind dredged up the negative moments of the past.

Soon, he was mired in the emotional roller coaster surrounding the tragedy that happened with his mother. Bitter thoughts clawed at his heart, and the muscles in his stomach tightened until he felt sick. Revolting scenes of a dark ravine made him want to cry out.

A blaring horn jolted him back to reality as a car swerved to miss him. Instinctively, he reached down and found a large rock to answer the rage within him. It fit neatly in the palm of his fist. Three years of frustration, pent-up anger, and hate propelled the weapon toward its target. The shattering sound of breaking glass surprised even him. The car skidded to a stop.

A. J. was shocked. It was not his intention to hit anything. Strangely, he felt neither sorrow nor regret, only continued rage. He would face whatever came.

An elderly gentleman emerged from the car and started toward A. J. Seeing the wild look in the boy's eyes and his clenched fists, he stopped. Without forcing the issue, he got back into the car to wait for help.

A. J. never moved until another vehicle did come along and stop. While two of the occupants stayed with the boy, a third drove to town to summon the police. Soon, A. J. dialed his father from the police station.

A. J. was uncomfortable in the courtroom atmosphere. Only four people were present in this new and strange environment. He studied the weathered face of the judge before the proceedings began. It wasn't a threatening look that met his eyes, but something different than he expected. Stern, maybe; but not threatening. A. J. was thankful for that.

Joe Franklin sat a couple of seats to the right of his son. Two seats on the other side of him, Mr. Larkin, the driver of the car he had damaged, waited patiently. Soon, Judge Evans's voice resonated in the chambers, commanding A. J.'s full attention.

"A. J." His pulse quickened as the judge spoke directly to him. "I've had a good visit with your father and Mr. Larkin before you came in. Their thoughts have helped me understand this situation. Before I say or think anything more, however, I'd like to hear your side of the story."

Fifteen seconds of silence seemed like a long time before A. J. responded.

"I don't really know. My day wasn't going well. My employer had just told me he wouldn't need me this summer. That seemed to magnify other problems. I was deep in thought, didn't really hear the car until it was there, and I guess I just got scared."

Another interval of silence shrouded the four until the judge spoke.

"What were you thinking about, son?"

Something about the tone in his voice spoke quietly to A. J. It was kind—no, it was more than kind. It was comforting and inviting. It was like the time he had abdominal pain and went with his mother to ol' Doc Roberts. The doctor had looked at him and said, "Tell me where it hurts, son."

A. J. stared at the floor with thoughts racing and colliding in his mind. *Does he really want to know what I am thinking? Can I really trust him?*

It was a much longer time of silence now. At length, A. J. slowly raised his head and looked at Judge Evans. Before he spoke, he blinked back tears that were rimming his eyes.

"That road I was walking on, Your Honor, is the same road that ..." his thoughts were coming too fast, and the words couldn't keep up. He needed his handkerchief to clear his vision. Again, an interval of silence.

"That's okay, A. J.," the judge said. "Take your time."

"Well, you know, my mother and I were in a terrible accident a few years ago. It was on that same road. So that's what I was thinking about the other day."

The boy paused again. A few more tears started to edge from his eyes. Judge Evans waited patiently.

"Then, without any warning, this car came hurtling around the curve, right into our lane. We had nowhere to go before it hit us. I guess the car rolled over—and over—and over ..." A. J.'s voice trailed off as he stared into the distance.

"Your mother was very special to you, wasn't she?"

"She was killed, Judge! She was killed! They said she had leaned over me to protect me! I lived! She died!"

"It's obvious your mother loved you very much." Judge Evans tried to console the grieving lad. "She would want you to know that."

A. J. breathed deeply and started to sob. Regaining composure, he looked intently at the judge.

"No, Judge, you don't understand. No one understands! We were on that road that night because *I* had stayed after school doing something *I* wanted to do. My mother came to pick me up. If it hadn't been for *me*, we would not have been on that road that night. We would not have been there when that other car went out of control. It's my fault!" he sobbed. "It's my fault she died!"

Exhausted, A. J. hid his head in his bent arms. The tears, like hot lava, continued to flow.

Three days later, the four met again. Judge Evans had formulated a plan. He perceived that A. J. had taken a big step in self-healing, but there was still a long way to go.

"A. J., you have already experienced a lot in your few short years, more than many youngsters your age. All of us here are aware of the difficult circumstances that caused you to do what you did. Because of this and your clean legal record in the past, we can be a little lenient.

"However, someone does have to pay for the broken window. And, although no one was physically injured in this accident, I want you to think about what could have happened. Mr. Larkin could have lost control of the car, injuring himself or perhaps even losing his life. There could have been another vehicle coming toward Mr. Larkin, and more people would have been involved."

The judge paused to give A. J. time to think about the incident.

"Do you see, young man, how one thoughtless action, even though it's unintentional, can cause irreparable damage?"

"Yes, Your Honor, I do. I'm sorry."

"Thankfully, the damage was minimal here. But you still need to make amends. My decision is that you will pay one hundred fifty dollars to Mr. Larkin to cover damages. In addition, I want you to give forty hours of your time helping someone in the community. Does that sound fair?"

"It sounds okay. But, like I mentioned the other day, I don't have a job right now," A. J. replied.

"Yes, I know. I can make some suggestions to help you fulfill these obligations. Do you mind if I do?"

"Not at all. That would be fine."

"You can think this over. To help you earn money, I can use someone here this summer to care for the grounds and do minor touch-up work inside the building. Concerning the volunteer hours, I know the school is having an outreach this summer tutoring school children. We could make arrangements for you to help there."

A. J. appeared thoughtful.

"Do you have any questions?" the judge asked.

"No, Your Honor."

"Okay. Thank you. I will wait to hear from you."

PART TWO

Whatever makes men good Christians,
makes them good citizens.
—Daniel Webster

No educated man can afford to be ignorant
of the Bible, and no uneducated man can
afford to be ignorant of the Bible.
—Theodore Roosevelt

It is harder to preserve than obtain liberty.
—John Caldwell Calhoun

Bridge Over
Troubled Waters

J udge Evans was elated that A. J. accepted his proposal because it gave him the opportunity to monitor the boy's progress. At the standard wage, A. J. would need most of the summer to earn enough money to pay for the window. After three days, the judge tried to strike up a friendly conversation with the boy.

"I notice you spend a lot of time in that circular room with all the sculptures. Find something interesting there?"

"Oh, not really," A. J. hedged.

"Well, if you have any questions, just ask. I've spent a lot of time raising money to build up the displays in that room."

"Oh, yeah? Well, they look nice."

A. J. felt cheap going home that evening. The truth was, he felt strangely comfortable in that room among the likenesses of George Washington, Patrick Henry, Ben Franklin, Abraham Lincoln, Thomas Jefferson, and others.

The sculptures weren't all that had caught his attention, however. He had also noticed some of the quotes shown, things these men had said. Especially one. But A. J. didn't want anyone to think he was actually interested. Nor did he want to appear stupid.

The summer reading program challenged A. J.'s creativity. He had been paired with a couple of ten-year-old boys. Fishing on a pond or playing baseball consumed their thoughts. A. J. tried to interest them with sports stories or outdoor magazines, but it seemed to be only a matter of going through the motions.

Spending morning hours with the boys made A. J. anxious to be back working at the courthouse. It was after one of those uninspiring mornings that the judge saw A. J. intently studying one of the busts in the circular room.

"Looks like more than just a passing interest." The judge's voice interrupted A. J.'s train of thought and startled the youngster.

"Oh, yeah. You know, this Patrick Henry guy, he sure had a lot of bravado making this boast: 'give me liberty or give me death!'" A. J. said protectively.

"Yes, he did."

The judge was more persistent this time.

"I'm sure you're aware that isn't the bust of Patrick Henry you're looking at."

"Oh, uh, yeah, sure; I know that."

"What is it about Abraham Lincoln that intrigues you so?"

A. J. looked back at the common replica of the sixteenth president and then again studied the plaque below it. He saw the futility of trying to bluff his mentor, so he came right to the point.

"It's this quote here. I know I've heard something similar before, somewhere—but I can't put my finger on it."

"What is the quote?"

Slowly, A. J. read it. "A house divided against itself cannot stand."

"No doubt you heard your teacher mention it at school."

"Well, yeah, I know that. But it was a completely different place than school. It seems so familiar, but I cannot put it together."

"Keep thinking about it. Sooner or later it will come to you. By the way, how's the tutoring coming?"

"Oh, it's all right, I guess," A. J. replied.

"That doesn't sound too convincing."

"They put me with two young boys who couldn't care less whether they are there or not."

"You're going to have to find their interests."

"I've tried that. All they're interested in is fishing or playing ball. I've gotten books on both subjects, but they're just not motivated to read."

"Maybe you need to read to them," the judge suggested.

"I've tried that too. Zero!"

"Well, maybe you need to try reading something different."

"Like what?"

The judge studied the surroundings for a few moments.

"Well, how about that man whose quote means so much to you?"

"Oh, like I'm sure history will grab them," A. J. said as he rolled his eyes.

"Well, no," the judge replied. "I don't mean the heavy stuff—something lighter."

A. J. laughed. "What's light about Lincoln?"

"How old are these boys?"

"Ten."

"I've got a great book on Lincoln's youth and teenage years. Why don't you take that and give it a try? Show them that side of the president. Wait here a second. I'll be right back."

A. J. was dubious about the suggestion. But he didn't want to hurt Judge Evans or dampen his enthusiasm. So when the judge returned with the book, he tried to muster a positive outlook.

Tucking the book under his arm, he managed a weak smile and said, "Well, I'll give it a try."

Three days later, A. J. hurried through lunch to get to the courthouse a few minutes early. Judge Evans sensed excitement in the young man even before he spoke. Hoping to further the boy's enthusiasm, the judge spoke first.

"So how's the summer reading going? You look like you've just won the Nobel Prize."

"That's a pretty good book you gave me, Judge. The boys are really picking up on it. It's hard for them to imagine that a president, especially one like Lincoln, was once a kid."

"I'll bet their favorite part was when Abe held up a youngster and made footprints on the ceiling of the cabin."

"Oh, they like that all right! And the time he won the wrestling match! And there are other things they are enjoying. But, you know, I don't think they're getting as much out of it as I am."

"Oh, really. How's that?"

"Well, for one, I know now where I heard that quote we were talking about."

"Really! How did you figure that out?"

"Well, you see, besides all the other boyhood things, the book tells how Abe liked to read so much. And then it tells how his mother encouraged him to read."

Judge Evans noticed A. J.'s voice soften, and his words come slower.

"It told how his mother would read to him from the Bible. All of a sudden, Judge, I was right there—back in my home as a youngster. Mom used to read to me from the Bible, just like Abe's mother read to him."

The quiet moments while A. J. brushed his eyes allowed the judge to collect his thoughts, but he never spoke.

"My mother loved to read from the Bible," the boy continued. "It was one of the most important things in her life. She wanted all of us to learn more about it. Sad to say, I didn't continue to read it the way she wanted me to. In fact, I haven't done much these past three years of what I used to do."

"Well, A. J., how does this tie in with that quote of Lincoln's?"

"This is it, Judge. It just became very clear to me, then, that this is where I heard it. Mom used to always read about Jesus, and Jesus is the one who said it."

"So you found it in the Bible?"

"No, no. Like I said, I haven't read the Bible like Mom wanted me to. I would have no idea where to even look. But I've got to find it, because ..."

"Because what?"

"Well, Judge, I don't get it. Lincoln was a president, right?"

"That's right."

"He was all about running a country. From what I know, Jesus wasn't interested in running countries. He had a clear different outlook on things."

"In a way, you're right," the judge said softly.

"Well, then, why would they both be saying the same thing—especially a quote like that?"

"That's a good question, son. There has to be an answer somewhere."

"I wish my mother was here so I could talk to her. She'd know."

"I'm sure she would. But some things just aren't possible. Isn't there someone else? How about your dad?"

"It's not quite the same talking with Dad about things like that. Besides, he is busy with his job and trying to keep the household things done. There's just so much on his mind that it's difficult to really get into a deep conversation."

"Maybe you need to give him more of a chance."

"Oh, we talk. But it's just not like—well, you know what I mean."

"Isn't there someone else you would feel comfortable with who would be helpful?"

"Jessie is away at college so that's not an option. The only other person I know who is a lot like Mom is Grandma Wilken. Not only do they act the same—they also think alike."

"Maybe you should pay her a visit."

"I haven't paid a lot of attention to her these past three years, Judge. I don't know how she would react to me now."

"I've known your grandma for thirty years. I've never known her to hold a grudge toward anyone, least of all her own kin. Just tell her you have a question and want to visit with her about it. If I know her like I think I do, I'll bet she'll even have freshly baked cinnamon rolls waiting for you."

Doubts

Aguarded smile dressed his face as A. J. inhaled the aroma of cinnamon rolls baking. Grandma Wilken welcomed him warmly with a hug that was halting, yet genuine.

"You surprised me with your phone call last night. I hope you like cinnamon rolls. They'll be ready in a few minutes."

"I was hoping you'd make some," A. J. replied. "You know they're my favorite. Thanks."

Grandma looked at him admiringly. "It's good to see you again. How is your summer going?"

"Oh, it's busy. I'm doing some volunteer work at the school, and also working at the courthouse for Judge Evans."

"Really?" Grandma seemed surprised. "What are you doing there?"

"I take care of the outside grounds and do touch-up work inside the building."

While A. J. made small talk, his grandmother took the finished rolls from the oven. She put two on a plate for her grandson and one for herself.

"There. What would you like to drink with that?" she asked.

"Cold milk would be great."

They took their rolls and drinks into the dining room where Grandma usually dined alone.

"Oh, these are good," said A. J. as he eagerly bit into the first one. "It's been a long time since I've had these."

"Yes, it has, A. J. And I miss the times we used to spend together."

"I know," said A. J. as he looked with compassion at his grandmother. "I want to apologize for the way I've been the last several years. It's just been—"

"I know, I know," she said. "We all truly miss your mother. I know how close the two of you were. It's difficult to lose a daughter. It's like part of me was ripped away." She paused. "And it's difficult to watch you suffer too."

"Grandma, about three weeks ago something happened in my life that made me stop and think. I don't know how much you know about it, but can I share it with you?"

"Why, certainly."

A. J. shared everything, in every detail that he could. Several times her hand found his and he squeezed hers in affirmation. He paused often, as they each wiped away tears. She never spoke until he was finished.

"I loved her so much, A. J. She was a beautiful person. I loved to see the relationship the two of you enjoyed. You know, she would have done anything for you."

"Yes, I know, and I feel guilty because she was taken while she was doing something for me."

"Think of it like this, A. J. If it was her time to go, she didn't have to die alone; she got to be with one of her children whom she loved so dearly."

The words penetrated A. J.'s mind and heart, but at the time, they were still just words. He changed the subject.

"Grandma, this wasn't the reason I came, but I'm glad we've had this talk."

"So am I, A. J."

"Well, anyway, Mom used to read to me out of the Bible."

Grandma's eyes took on a new sparkle.

"I've come across a saying lately that reminded me of this. I have to admit I haven't read much since the accident, let alone the Bible. I know this saying is from the Bible because I remember Mom reading it. But I have no idea where to find it."

"What is it?"

"'A house divided against itself cannot stand.' I think Jesus said it."

"Yes, you're right. Jesus did say that."

"Well, what did he mean? Why did he say it?"

"That's a long story, but it's a very interesting story. It would be best if we read about it first and then discussed it."

A. J. glanced at his watch.

"I guess I used too much time talking about my other experiences. I'd like to get to bed in good time this evening because I have an appointment early in the morning."

"Well, that's okay. Can you come back sometime?" his grandma asked.

"Sure, I could do that. Would Friday evening work for you?"

"Friday would be perfect. In the meantime, I'll show you some helpful verses in the Bible. You can read them before you come back. You do have your Bible, don't you?"

"I guess it's somewhere," A. J. said sheepishly, "but I'd have to find it."

"Here, you can borrow this one. I have others. Now, I'll put a marker in three places. There are other references, but this will help you get started."

"Thanks a lot. Hey, I enjoyed our visit, Grandma. See you Friday about seven o'clock."

"I enjoyed it too, A. J. Don't forget to read those sections I marked."

A. J. met his grandmother Friday evening with loads of questions. After a few minutes of small talk, he was ready to get to the issues at hand.

"I'm assuming you read those sections I suggested, A. J. What did you think?"

"It wasn't what I expected, Grandma."

"Oh, really? What did you expect?"

"I don't know what I expected. But all of those readings had one thing in common."

"And what was that?"

"Each one talked about people who had devils in them, and Jesus cast the devils out of them."

"Yes, that's correct. Is that confusing to you?"

A. J. hesitated before answering.

"Well, yeah! I mean it sounds like science fiction or something."

A. J. furrowed his brow while looking at Grandma.

"Do you think that really happened?"

"Yes, I do," Grandma said softly.

"Why? Where did these devils come from in the first place?" A. J. looked puzzled as he stared off into space.

"You're asking some pretty deep questions, A. J. It will take a while to discuss them."

"I've got time this evening if you do, Grandma."

"Okay. Let's get some iced tea and cookies first. Then we'll really get started."

The seasoned lady and the energetic lad sat around a circular wooden table. A chandelier above the table highlighted the open Bibles. A. J. took a bite of the warm cookie and washed it down with iced tea. He waited for Grandma to begin.

"I've found during my lifetime, A. J., that whenever I have a problem or a lot of questions, it helps to find a good starting point.

In this case, we're going to be talking about spiritual things, so let's go back to the beginning when God started it all."

"I can tell right away that you're going to have to walk me pretty slowly through this. A lot of times I've thought about where it all begins, but I can't figure it out."

"Neither can I, A. J.," his grandmother said in her gentle voice. "But the best record we have is the Bible. We can find enough in there to help us understand what we need to know."

"You know, Grandma, you sound so much like Mom. It feels good just being here."

Mrs. Wilken found it difficult to respond. She just nodded her head several times while reaching for a tissue.

"Thank you, A. J. You don't know how much that means to me."

After composing herself, she said, "Well, the first book of the Bible is Genesis. That book tells us that God created everything."

"I have a question right away, then."

"Good. What is it?"

"If God created everything, did he also create the devils Jesus was dealing with?"

"You have good reasoning power, son. Do you mind if I call you son sometimes?"

"No, that's okay. In fact, I like it."

"You are good at picking up details. And that is an excellent question. I guess we'd say yes and no."

"Yes and no? Wow, this is getting confusing."

"You see, God created the angels, and the devils were angels at one time."

"I've never read that!"

"That's very possible. It's not in Genesis. It's probably not something you would hear very often. But as we read through the Bible there are references that talk about it."

"Could you show me one?" A. J. asked.

"Sure. Let's turn to the book of Nehemiah. That's one of the smaller books of the Old Testament. Here, I'll help you find it."

"Okay," A. J. said as they found the verse. "You read, and I'll follow along."

"All right, turn to chapter nine. Verse six of that chapter says, 'Thou, even thou, art Lord alone; thou hast made heaven, the heaven of heavens, with all their host, the earth, and all things that are therein, the seas, and all that is therein, and thou preservest them all; and the host of heaven worshippeth thee.'"

"Well," A. J. said after a few moments. "I guess that says a lot. God did create everything, even the angels."

Grandma remained quiet while the boy thought about it.

"Okay, then," the youngster replied, "you said that the devils were once angels. What happened?"

"Evidently, God gave the angels different positions and different duties. One of the angels had very special duties. This angel was very beautiful and was known as the Angel of Light."

"I've never really thought of things this way before. I just thought heaven was a place above us with not much happening."

"It's easy to do that, I know," said Grandma. "We get so involved with our lives here on earth that we forget God has another creation in heaven."

"This is exciting," the young man mused. "But it's also hard to believe. Do you ever feel that way?"

"Yes, I guess there are times like that. But that is what we call faith; when we believe things that we cannot see."

A. J. thought about this for a while. Then he wanted to continue.

"Okay, then what happened to this special angel?"

"Well, he became very proud. He wanted to be more important than he really was. In fact, he wanted to become equal with God."

"Was he allowed to do that?"

"No. You see, pride is one thing God cannot tolerate. Even when we become proud of what we can do, or our accomplishments, or whatever, God cannot use us."

"So this angel lost his position, I bet," ventured A. J.

"Worse than that. There must have been quite a struggle because it ended with God casting him out of heaven."

"The angel was actually thrown out of heaven?"

"Yes. Look here in the gospel of Luke. Jesus was talking to his disciples and he said, 'I beheld Satan as lightning fall from heaven.'"

A. J. was silent for a couple of minutes while he thought about the things he had read and heard. When he spoke again, it was with a quieter voice.

"So that was how Satan got to earth, right?"

"That's right. Remember how I said there was a struggle in heaven?"

"Yes," he answered.

"It must have been a tremendous struggle. A struggle for the ages, because when Satan fell, he dragged one-third of the angels with him."

"When did all this happen?"

"That's one thing we don't know," said Grandma. "But we do know it was before man was created."

"How do we know that?"

"Because Satan was present in the Garden of Eden when Adam and Eve lived there."

"I remember Mom reading that story to me."

"Yes. Satan became the enemy of God. He saw that God had made a wonderful creation on earth. He knew that God loved the man and woman he had created. So he caused the man and woman to disobey God, knowing that would put a barrier between them and God."

"Didn't God do anything about that?"

"Yes, he did. First, he had to remove the man and woman from the beautiful garden because they had sinned. God cannot tolerate sin."

"Well, haven't we sinned, Grandma?"

"Yes, we have, but you're getting ahead of me here. After that, God made a promise that He would send a Redeemer, meaning someone who would come to redeem, or buy back, that which He had lost."

A. J. stared at the table. Only the ticking of the mantel clock could be heard. After a long interval, he looked up.

"I think this is going to take more than just a night or two. Can I have a few days to think about all of this?"

"Okay. Yes, that is quite a lot to think about. Just give me a call when you're ready again. I'm free most evenings."

As her grandson walked down the walk, Mrs. Wilken hoped she hadn't said anything to discourage his search. Those last moments of silence were troubling. The light in his eyes seemed a little dimmer than when the evening had begun.

"Judge," A. J. asked, his voice entreating, "are you a student of the Bible?"

"I read it quite regularly. Why?"

"Well, as you might guess, Grandma knows it well, and she is way over my head."

"She's quite a bit older than you, so you can expect that. I suspect she knows and understands the Bible far better than most people her age. She's been a devoted disciple for many years."

"Do you believe everything that is in the Bible?" A. J. raised his eyebrows, waiting for the judge to ponder and respond.

"A. J., you remind me of myself when I was your age. I didn't read it a lot, didn't care too much about Sunday school or church, and I questioned most of what I heard from other people about the Bible and God."

"It sounds like you've changed your mind."

"Yes, I have."

"When did that happen? Why?"

"I started to read it more, just like you are now. And, oh, I had a multitude of questions and doubts. Then I went to college and began studying law and history. I began to see where a lot of statesmen like those represented by the statues and pictures in this room would often quote the Bible."

"Did all famous people like the Bible?"

"Oh no, not at all! There are many who tried to disprove the Bible. I read about them too."

"How did you come to a conclusion, then, to believe the Bible?"

"When I finished school and started in this profession, I rubbed shoulders with people from all walks of life. Just by being observant and studying characteristics of people, I began to feel that the words of Jesus pointed to the greatest attributes anyone could possess to live a fulfilling life," the judge explained.

"You really believe that, don't you?"

"With all my heart. And when I fully turned my life over to the power of God, it changed my outlook on everything. I can't imagine doing this job any other way."

Judge Evans watched A. J.'s reflective eyes again.

"Grandma was talking about something the other day that is difficult for me to comprehend. She said Jesus was casting devils out of people."

"Yes, I'm familiar with that."

"Do you believe that? That there really were devils?"

"Oh, sure," the older man responded.

A. J. stared incredulously.

"When did they disappear?"

"Who says they disappeared?"

"Now, hold on a minute. You're implying that devils are still around today. How do you know?"

"Well, I can't say I have ever seen one. But I see the effects of evil nearly every day. That's part of my job that I have to deal with."

"Okay! If you say you have never seen one, how can you say devils exist?"

"There are things written in the Bible no one will be able to prove. That is where faith comes in."

"Faith?"

"Yes. Having faith is believing something without actually seeing it. God says we need to have faith to be one of his children."

"Isn't that asking a lot, to believe something without visible evidence?"

"I guess you could look at it that way. But even your man Lincoln said this to a friend about the Bible: 'Take all you can of this Book on reason, and the rest by faith, and you will live and die a happier man.'"

A profound silence followed the judge's last statement. After allowing time for the silence to punctuate the message, Judge Evans dismissed himself.

"I need to meet my wife in fifteen minutes. Would you lock up before you leave?"

"Oh, uh, sure. Have a nice weekend. I'll see you Monday."

A MESSAGE FROM BEYOND

After nearly a week without hearing from A. J., Grandma wanted to talk things over with Judge Evans.

"I waited until evening to call you at home," she explained. "I didn't want A. J. to become suspicious in case he was working with you today. Have you seen him lately?"

"Yes, I have. In fact, I just left him this afternoon to close the office. He has become quite responsible this summer. He does seem to be weighing some things very carefully, almost to the point of distraction."

"That's kind of what I thought might be happening. You know, it's been almost a week since I have talked with him. I mentioned to you the other day my concerns when he left last Friday evening."

"He shared with me some of your conversation, Grandma, and asked some very intriguing questions. Were you surprised at all with his questions to you?"

"No, not surprised. I am delighted that he is asking questions. My only fear, like I already mentioned, is that it was too much too fast," Grandma Wilken replied.

"I know what you mean. Well, what do you suggest?"

"Do you remember what I shared with you and Doc Roberts about six months ago? I don't want to get more descriptive than that over the phone."

"Yes, I think I know what you are talking about."

"I feel now is the time to talk to him about it."

"That very thought was on my mind also. I'm glad you brought it up. If you hadn't, I might have suggested it. But you are certainly the one in charge of that."

"How do you think Doc would feel about it?"

"I'm sure he would agree. In fact, when we were talking the other day, he thought that might be the best thing for him," the judge responded.

"Well, I'm encouraged since both of you feel as I do. Now, I just have to wait for him to call—and hope he is still in a mood to talk."

The following Monday, A. J. did contact her. He suggested meeting at the restaurant downtown, confirming Grandma's fears that the young man didn't want to continue the studies they had begun.

"Well, A. J., I was hoping you would come here. I want to make a cherry pie and I'll get some ice cream to go with it."

There was silence while A. J. tried to think of something. The treat did sound inviting, but it wasn't in his plans.

"I guess maybe I could come there. I wasn't planning on staying long, though."

"That's okay. When do you want to get together?"

"Tomorrow after work would be fine with me. I could be there about four thirty."

"Four thirty it is. I'll have the pie and ice cream waiting."

"What can I get you to drink with the pie a la mode?" Grandma asked cheerily.

"This is going to be sweet enough," responded A. J. "I think a glass of ice water will be fine."

A. J. took his first bite. Mrs. Wilken set the ice water before him.

"Oh, this is good. You didn't need to do this, Grandma, but I'm glad you did."

Mrs. Wilken chuckled. "Like they say, there's nothing too good for my grandson."

"Thanks, Grandma. You know, you're the best."

A serious expression met the older woman the next time A. J. looked up.

"Grandma, I've had a tough week. I'm just so confused. I'm afraid I've lost so much these past three years that I don't know if I can ever catch up."

"What's troubling you, A. J.?"

"Well, part of it is what we read together the other day. I don't know, all this about devils and everything—I mean, I'm just not used to thinking like that. And Judge Evans, we've been talking about it too. He says you need faith to believe some things. How do you get faith, anyway? And then, while I'm thinking about all this, my mind goes back to the accident and everything gets blurry again. I just don't know."

Mrs. Wilken listened carefully. When there was a few moments' pause, she tried to answer him.

"No one expects you to receive more than what you can handle. But it appears that your heart and mind are ready to expand your thinking."

"Why do you say that?"

"You've got these questions that you want answered. And when we receive new information, it takes time to digest it."

Grandma studied him while he finished the pie and gave him time to think about what she had said.

"A. J.," Mrs. Wilken said softly, trying to sound natural. "There's something I think you should know."

The tone of her voice didn't escape his attention. Like a deer hearing crackling twigs, he studied her face carefully.

"Your mother was an amazing person, A. J."

"Yes, I know that," he said matter-of-factly, while standing up.

"Through all of her goodness, she had one overriding concern."
A. J. stood motionless. Hesitantly, Loretta's mother continued.
"The welfare of you and Jessie dominated her actions."
Grandma paused a few moments before continuing.

"Her greatest fear, like many parents I suppose, was that she would not be around to help the two of you become adults."

"You mean," A. J. asked with a look of disbelief, "she had a—a premonition of her death?"

"Let's just say her love touched all possibilities."

"I don't understand," he stammered. "What do you mean?"

Only the steady ticking of the mantel clock could be heard as Mrs. Wilken reached into her apron pocket. She handed a sealed envelope to A. J.

"Your mother wrote a letter to each of you when you were about ten years old. Of course, she hoped it would never have to be given to you. She wanted to be able to see both of you grown. But, if that was not the case, she still wanted to help you."

"This ... this is from Mom?"

"Yes, it is, A. J."

"But that was years ago!"

"I know. She gave it to your father and me, in case anything unforeseen would happen to her, to give to you when we thought you could handle it. As time went by, your father wanted me to make that decision."

Grandma paused. Then cupping her hands around his, she said, "I think that time has now come."

When she released her hold, A. J.'s hands were shaking. A letter from his mother! Written in her own hand! He wanted to open it quickly. Yet it felt like such a reverent moment that all he could do was press it close to him.

He sat down at the dining table. As the quiet moments slipped by, he gently placed the envelope on the table. Resting his head on his hands, he longingly stared at the beautiful handwriting: *Aaron Joseph*.

The young man felt a hand softly on his shoulder, like a butterfly lighting on a flower. Her gentle voice floated to him.

"I'll be in the kitchen if you need me, A. J."

And then, he was alone.

Dear Aaron,

Since the day you were born, my fondest wish has been to be able to enjoy life with you and your beautiful sister, Jessie, along with your loving father. We both want happiness and fulfillment for your lives. Above all, we want you to become clothed with the righteousness of our Savior.

God has intended good things for us. Sometimes, however, life can be difficult. Sometimes things don't work out the way we thought they would. I don't know what the future holds any more than anyone else. But if you are reading this letter, God must have seen fit to take me home to Him.

The Lord sprinkled a lot of love in our lives when He gave you and Jessie to us. The day you were born, son, we did not have a name picked out yet for you. The name Aaron kept coming to me. I didn't know why. Now I think I understand.

In the Bible, Aaron was used by God to be a spokesperson for Moses. A.J., you have been given a wonderful gift of communication. If you give yourself into God's service, He will use you in a mighty way. What you are when you are young is God's gift to you; what you become as you age is your gift to God.

Not many things in this life are perfect. But the Bible does speak of the "perfect law of liberty." Like all laws, there are rules to help you achieve the fulfillment of that law. My sincere hope is that you will discover the rules that lead you to this perfect law.

There is so much I would want to say to you and give you, but if you find the perfect law of liberty, you will have found the fullness of my heart's desire for you.

With all my love,
Mom

A. J. stared at the mantel clock as though he could will it to take him back in time. He gazed out the window into the mist of years gone by. He couldn't comprehend what he held in his hands.

Then he read the letter again, and again—five times. He carefully put it back into the envelope, took a deep breath, and rushed to the kitchen.

"Grandma," he said, his voice cracking with emotion. "I've got to talk to her!"

Before Mrs. Wilken could react, he was out the door, racing on his bicycle to the church just outside of town.

A. J. breathed deeply, allowing the cool, fresh air to cleanse his body. When nearly to the church, he could see the form of someone in the cemetery. He didn't think it strange that someone would be visiting a loved one's grave. Getting closer, however, he realized that the person appeared to be in the vicinity of that sacred spot. Then he was sure of it; the person was standing by his mother's grave.

He dropped the bicycle on its side and quickly dismounted while he called to the visitor. It wasn't possible to get a good look at the man who briefly turned and then quickly darted away. The man did look vaguely familiar, like someone from a book he had read a long time ago.

Adrenaline kicked in, and the boy gave chase. Just as it seemed he was gaining on the man, A. J. stumbled and fell. He slammed his fist to the ground; he realized he could never catch the intruder now. He slowly raised himself and walked back to his mother's grave.

A. J. fell to his knees and then stretched out with his face toward the ground, exhausted. Like a broken levy, sobs and tears clothed his verbal reminisces.

"I miss you so much," he stammered. "If I could just see you one more time! If only it could be like it was before!"

For a long time, the teenager lay prostrate on the ground. Then he slowly got to his knees.

"Mom, it's been miserable without you. There's nothing I wouldn't do to have you back." It seemed strange to A. J. to do all the talking. "But I know it's not possible to have you back." He paused. "So I'll try to do the best I can. Grandma is like you. She's trying so hard to help me. And Dad and Jessie are great."

As he came to his knees, a bouquet of fresh cut flowers in a copper vase caught his eye.

"Mom, these flowers remind me of you. I wish you could have heard the wonderful things people from Bridges said about you at the graveside service. I'll have to thank Grandma for remembering you with these flowers."

Looking at the inscription of his mother's name on the headstone, he groaned and then continued speaking.

"Thanks for the letter, Mom. I got it today. Just knowing it's from you and seeing your handwriting—well, I'll treasure it forever."

One more time, A. J. cried, allowing the tears to flow unhindered. Then he dried his eyes and stood up. "I don't fully understand right now some of the things you wrote, like liberty and the perfect law."

A. J. took his time. He was in no hurry to leave. "But if you think it's important, Mom, I will work till I find it. With someone's help, I will find it, and I will make you happy!"

A New Beginning

The yellowish-orange sun hung like a giant grapefruit in the western sky, inching closer to the horizon with a reddish-orange hue. A. J. slowed his bicycle. Home was just around the bend. The beautiful sunset accentuated his peaceful mood. The warmth of his mother's words seeped through his clothes and skin and massaged his heart. He parked his bike, and he savored the moments before walking up the porch steps.

"You've had two phone calls this evening," his father said.

"Two?"

"Your sister called earlier. She would like you to call her when you can."

"Is she still at school?"

"Yes. She'll be awake until about ten o'clock."

"Who was the other call? I usually don't get two calls in one evening."

"That was your grandmother. She just wanted to know if you made it home okay."

"Okay. I'll call her right away."

A. J. started toward the kitchen and then stopped.

"Dad," he said. "Have you got a few spare minutes? After I make this call, I'd like to tell you about today."

"Sure, son. I need a break anyway. I'll be in the den room."

He assured his grandmother everything was fine, and then he joined his father in the den.

"I visited the cemetery today, Dad."

"Oh! That's interesting," his father said with a quizzical look.

"Why do you think anyone would have been standing by Mom's grave?"

"Oh, I don't know," his father responded. "Some people occasionally walk through cemeteries searching for historical value. They may stop to check the dates on headstones or something like that."

"I never thought of that." A. J. paused a few moments. "What seemed funny, though, was that the moment he heard me and saw me, he took off running. I tried to chase him."

"Did you catch him?"

"No." A. J. chuckled. "I stumbled and fell because I was so tired from riding the bike. It just seemed strange, him running like that."

"You're right. That is strange. Very strange, indeed. I have no clue what he might have been doing."

Joe looked intently at his son before continuing.

"But what interests me more right now is why you were there."

"Are you sure you want to know?"

"Why, of course. I've got time to listen."

A. J. recounted the day's events, beginning with his visit to Grandma and the reason he went to see her. He never forgot a detail. It was the warmest discussion he enjoyed with his father in a long time. They wept together, and neither one was ashamed. A friendship reignited that evening in a room where laughter and love had once reigned supreme, but lately had been devoid of warmth. Each of them knew that the past could not be recaptured. But each of them also knew that things could be, and would be, better than they had been.

"A. J., would it be okay if we prayed together?" his father asked cautiously.

"I'd like nothing better right now, Dad."

Together, they knelt in that little room while Joe implored the Spirit of God to lead them in prayer.

"Blessed Father, we feel unworthy of Thy love and grace. Yet we believe Thou dost love us. We are encouraged in Thy word that we should always pray. We're thankful we can together come to Thee in this manner. It has been so difficult losing our beloved wife and mother. We're trying to understand and continue on in this life. Help us to see what you would have us do. Remember Jessie, who is in school many miles away from us. Help her in her studies. We thank Thee for Grandma Wilken and all she is doing for us. Bless her, dear Father. Now, would'st Thou be with A. J.? Direct him, O Father, with Thy Spirit. If there is a special calling awaiting him, help him to be humble and to follow Thy direction. There is so much we should pray for, but sometimes we don't even know what that is. We only ask yet for Thy guidance and protection. In the blessed name of Jesus, we pray. Amen."

Getting back to their feet, they stood silently for a few moments. Then they shared the warmest embrace they had shared since the accident.

"You'd better call your sister, son. She's anxious to talk with you."

"Thanks, Dad. I'll use the phone in the kitchen."

"Hey, Jess, what's up?" A. J. asked when his sister answered the phone.

"Oh, hi, A. J. Thanks for calling back."

"No problem," he responded.

"Did Dad tell you why I called?"

"No, he just said you wanted me to get back to you this evening."

"Okay. I was wondering if you've thought any more about next year."

"Next year? What do you mean?"

"Well, you will be starting your senior year next week, right?"

"Yes."

"Are you thinking about going to school somewhere after you graduate?"

"Things have been so busy and exciting this summer that I simply haven't thought much about it."

"A. J.," Jessie said with a degree of hesitation. "Do you mind if I ask you a question?"

"No, not at all. Go ahead."

"Well, you seem … different. I can hear it in your voice. Something has happened, hasn't it?"

"Jess, I don't know how to describe it. Today has been the most, uh, fantastic day, I guess you might say, that I've had in a long time."

"Can you share it with me?" Jessie asked eagerly.

"Oh, it would take too long to tell everything over the phone. I don't want to run up the bill for Dad. He has enough expense the way it is."

"Well, can you give me some idea of what happened?"

"Sure. I'll try to hit some of the high points."

With that, A. J. briefly explained some of the major happenings of the day. When he was finished, she was quiet.

"Are you still there, Jess?"

"What? Oh, yes."

"Jessie, did you also get a letter from Mom?"

The young lady hesitated.

"Yes, I did, A. J."

"Did you get yours before now?"

"Well, yes, I did. But, you see, I wasn't as directly involved in the accident as you were and—"

"That's okay, Jess. I figured you did. You know, I don't think I could have handled it if I had received it before now. I think Grandma knew exactly what she was doing when she waited to give it to me."

Jessie hurried to change the subject before this dream-world bubble burst.

"Before we use up too much time, I want to get back to the reason I called."

"Okay, go ahead."

"You see, my roommate, Sharon, is the daughter of our university president."

"Wow! How did you arrange that?"

"That's just the way it happened."

"Do you like that?"

"Oh, it's terrific. She's as sweet as the day is long. I've been invited many times to their home for a meal."

"Is she also a senior?"

"As a matter of fact, she is. We'll both graduate next spring if everything goes well. Anyway, she told me that an open house is being planned for sometime in October. Anyone interested in attending school here next year is invited."

"So you think I should begin to explore my options?"

"Exactly."

Jessie waited a few anxious moments for a reply.

"You know, Jess, that might not be a bad idea. It's probably about time I started making some positive plans for my life."

"Great. I'll let you know the dates when I find out more."

"Okay. Oh, one other thing. Can Dad and Grandma come too?"

"Sure, A. J. I think that's a great idea."

"Okay. You get the dates for us, and we'll put it on our calendars."

"Thanks, A. J. I'll get back to you as soon as I can."

"Are you okay, Jessie? You almost sound like you're crying."

"Oh, no, A. J. I'm fine. Really! Just fine."

A. J.'s spiritual reconnection with his mother lifted him to a higher plane. Grandma noticed it immediately when they met the following week.

"Your dad told me about your experiences last Thursday," she said. "It sounds like you had a wonderful day."

"Thanks to you, Grandma, it was one of the best days I've had in a long time."

"I was only doing what the Lord told me to do, A. J. The thanks belongs to Him, and to you for responding the way you did."

"You never take any credit for yourself, do you, Grandma? I guess that's why you're able to help so many people. And your daughter turned out just like you."

"We're all just instruments, son. We need to be ready to be used when the Lord asks us."

"I guess you figured out that I had no intention of continuing our studies when I came to see you last week."

"Yes. I had been afraid that was in your mind."

"Well, let me tell you that now I am more enthused than ever. I want to find what Mom was talking about. I want to make her happy. Oh, here, I'll let you read the letter."

Grandma took the letter and cautiously opened it. Eagerly, but slowly, she read it, pausing only once to ask her grandson for a handkerchief. When she finished reading, she put it back in the envelope and handed it to A. J.

"That's quite a treasure you have there."

"Oh, I know! It has become a part of me, of what I want to be. Are you familiar with what she wrote about the perfect law of liberty?"

"Oh, yes."

"Is it written in the Bible?"

"Yes, it is."

"We could read that, then, together," A. J. said enthusiastically.

"Yes, we could. But you see, reading it and experiencing it are two different things. Your mother found it, she experienced it, and that's what she wants for you, to truly experience that law."

The young man gazed reflectively out the window, and then turned back to his grandmother.

"Will you help me find it?"

"I'll do what I can."

"When can we begin?"

"Tomorrow evening, if it works for you."

"It works for me," A. J. said as he hugged her and reached for the door.

As he stepped out on the porch, he turned back with one last thought.

"Oh, I almost forgot. While I was kneeling at Mom's grave last week, I saw all those beautiful, fresh-cut flowers. It reminded me of all the nice things that were said by the people at her graveside service. I wanted to be sure to thank you for taking those flowers to her grave."

Grandma looked up with a puzzled expression on her face.

"Flowers?" she said. "I didn't put any fresh flowers on her grave last week."

DEEP WATERS

A. J. looked across the town square as he sat on the steps of the courthouse, and he reflected upon the happenings of the past summer. Three months ago, he had trudged up these same steps, wary of what awaited him. Today, he cringed at the thought that it was coming to an end.

The door opened slowly behind him, and he heard the voice that had helped him mature beyond his years.

"Oh, there you are. I was hoping you would come today. I've got a lot of papers that need filing."

The boy stood and turned to face the older gentleman. Tears rimmed his eyes as he reached out to shake his hand. The hand-clasp quickly evolved into a tender embrace lasting several seconds.

"I'm going to miss you, A. J.," the judge whispered. "You're like one of my own. I'm sure going to miss you."

Too emotional to speak, A. J. silently entered the courthouse building with his friend. They walked into the judge's spacious office.

"Are there tasks yet that need to be done?" A. J. asked. "I'd like to keep coming here after school hours."

"Oh, there are always things that need to be done. But I imagine you will be kept quite busy with your studies, football, basketball, and other things."

"I think I can handle the studies okay. As for the other activities, I don't believe I'm going to include them."

"You're not?" The judge seemed surprised. "It sounds to me like the coaches are looking forward to you playing this year."

"Yeah, I know. But things are changing."

The judge motioned for the boy to pull up a chair on one side of his old oak table. He pulled up a chair on the other side, facing him. The older gentleman listened.

"If I had started playing football and basketball as a freshman, I know I would be just as excited as some of my classmates. Sure, I think it's important to interact with others like that, and I'm all for them. That's good."

Judge Evans nodded as the boy continued.

"But right now, I'm feeling a tug from a different direction. Those things that my mother told me in that letter have captured my entire being."

"What things in particular?"

"Liberty. I'm fascinated with that word. I cannot believe how many times I have noticed it since reading Mom's letter."

"It is a powerful word and a tremendous concept," the judge added. "I deal with it often, either granting it to someone or taking it away."

"I never thought of that. You do, don't you?"

The judge noticed A. J.'s fascination.

"I have a few happy moments when I can pardon someone who is truly innocent." His slight smile dissolved. "It seems, however, there are more unhappy moments than happy ones, such as when I have to pronounce a judgment that takes liberty away from a youngster or even an older person."

A long period of silence followed. A. J.'s voice finally broke the stillness.

"Why is that, Judge? Why do people so carelessly throw away something that precious?"

"I don't know, son. I don't know. I've been at this business about forty years and I still can't explain it." He got out of his chair and slowly walked to the window overlooking the square. "The only thing I can figure out is that a lot of people don't understand freedom. They don't realize what they have until they lose it."

A. J. pondered Judge Evans's words before responding. "I guess in America we just grow up taking it for granted, don't we?"

"Yes, I'm afraid we do. It's too bad. That which we don't value highly, we risk losing."

The judge turned away from the window and directed his words toward A. J. again. "We're not studying our history the way we should. We're forgetting our roots."

"When you say *we*, who do you mean?"

"I mean our nation as a whole, especially the younger generation. It seems the further we get away from our beginning, the less we remember how things were. It's like you just said, we're taking our liberty for granted. Lincoln said it best: 'If we knew from whence we came, we could better tend to where we are going.'"

A. J.'s pulse quickened. He wanted to respond but felt inadequate in the presence of his mentor. He hoped the judge would continue. After a few moments of reflective meditation, the judge obliged him.

"Son, our nation fought two internal wars to get us where we are today. The first coincided with our Declaration of Independence, freeing us from British tyranny. The second was the big war that freed the rest of our country's inhabitants from bondage."

Again, a sharp silence penetrated the room before the judge punctuated his speech. "We must never forget! We must never allow our people to forget, either!"

"A. J., you're early! Or am I behind schedule?" Grandma asked while opening the door.

"No, I just had plenty of time this evening so I thought I'd drop over a little early."

"Come in. I'll need about twenty minutes to finish these cookies. They'll be hot out of the oven for you then."

"Grandma, you're always spoiling me."

"Well, I can't think of anything better to do," she replied.

A. J. started looking through the large collection of books in the library room.

"Oh, A. J.," she called. "Would you run upstairs and get that old family Bible? It might come in handy later. You'll find it on the small table in the old farm room."

The youngster was glad for the opportunity to visit the room he had stayed in many times years ago. Life seemed simple then; he cherished the feeling of security and coziness of staying at Grandma's. The slightly faded wallpaper was beginning to curl at the corners. Farm animals and tractors on the paper seemed smaller now.

He found the table with the family Bible on it. An irresistible urge gripped him to open it. Grandma had scribbled notes on many pages and circled important things she wanted to remember. Continuing to turn the pages, he soon arrived at the Family Record page.

Magnetically, his eyes were drawn to the name *Loretta Franklin*. He quickly noted the date of her birth and the date of her death. The name of Loretta's brother was two lines above hers, and her sister's name appeared one line below his. Both of them were gone also. At the top of the page was the wedding date of his grandmother and grandfather. He located another entry bearing the date of his grandfather's death, two years before A. J. was born.

On the bottom third of the page, he noticed the wedding date of Joe and Loretta Franklin. This was followed by the births of Jessie and A. J. He pondered those dates, whispering to himself, "We're all Grandma has left—Dad, Jessie, and me! She has lost her spouse and all three of her children!"

Twenty minutes passed quickly. Soon he and his grandmother sat at the table, delving into the sacred word.

"Well, A. J., do you have any lingering questions from when we met before?"

"As a matter of fact, I do, Grandma. I've read and studied those verses you gave me the first time."

"And?"

"I still have a tough time accepting it all."

"Accepting what?" Grandma asked with a disappointing look.

"All of this casting out devils business. I just don't see it."

"How about if we go over those verses again?"

"Whatever you think best, Grandma."

The better part of an hour found the two scholars reviewing dramatic examples of Jesus casting out devils in different situations.

"Did this happen often?" A. J. asked at one point.

Then Grandma would turn to another scripture just as dramatic as the one before it. The last one she talked about involved Mary Magdalene.

"I have heard about her," A. J. exclaimed. "This other stuff seems pretty foreign, but I have heard her name used."

"Yes," Grandma spoke with an excited tone. "Jesus cast seven devils out of her, and she became one of His devoted followers."

A. J. stood up to stretch. He slowly paced around the room and then came back to his side of the table.

"Grandma," he said, measuring his words carefully, "do you really think all of this actually happened, or are we reading into it what we want to think? I mean, it … it all seems so fantastic."

"Well," Grandma slowly responded, "I think the answer to your question leads us directly to your original question. But, you know, we've been talking about some pretty deep things here. Let's take a break and get some iced tea with those fresh cookies, okay?"

"Sounds super! I'll pour the tea while you get the cookies."

"Here are some peaches to go with those cookies and iced tea. Let's just sit back and relax awhile."

"Oh, Granny, this is a terrific snack. Thanks a bunch."

She looked at her grandson admiringly.

"That's the first time you've called me that since ... well, I can't remember how long. It sure brings back good memories of years gone by."

That kindled an atmosphere of reminiscing. They recalled pleasant times about Loretta while enjoying their refreshments. When he was finished, A. J. pushed back in the soft recliner. Staring at the painted ceiling, he broached another topic.

"Grandma, tell me about your other children."

Mrs. Wilken was taken by surprise. "Whatever makes you think of them?"

"I saw their names in the family Bible while I was upstairs."

"I wondered what was taking you so long."

"Mom never talked a lot about them."

"It seems like a long time ago." Grandma sighed.

"You had two other children, right? A boy and a girl?"

"That's correct. Edward Jr., named after his father, was four years older than Loretta. Sarah was the middle child, two years younger than Edward and two years older than Loretta."

"So Mom was the youngest?"

"Yes."

The soft chimes of the clock made the conversation comfortable.

"Were they good friends, or did Mom get left out a lot since she was the youngest?"

"That's an interesting question. But, yes, they were very kind to each other. Oh, they had their little spats and disagreements, but basically they played well together."

"There was the same age difference, wasn't there, between Edward and my mother as there is between Jessie and me?"

"Four years, yes. But you and Jessie always got along well."

"I know, but there are only two of us. I didn't know if a third person would make a difference, especially for the youngest one."

"It didn't seem to. You know, other than size, there didn't seem to be a big difference among them. Loretta was always mature beyond her years. She was probably the most mature of them all."

"What happened to them, Grandma?"

"We lost our little Sarah when she was fourteen. She took ill with pneumonia, and we couldn't pull her out of it. Eddie lost his life in France during World War II."

The house was silent except for the ticking of the old mantel clock. A couple of minutes may have gone by before A. J. brought his chair back to a sitting position. He smiled while looking at his grandmother.

"Grandma," he said in a strong whisper, "you've lost your husband and all three children. How do you do it?"

"How do I do what?"

"You're always so … so upbeat, so cheerful, when you have reasons to be down. How do you always stay so pleasant?"

Kindness spilled from Grandma's heart as she answered his question.

"I couldn't do it, A. J., on my own."

"What do you mean, Grandma?"

"I couldn't do it without the power and presence of God."

The ticking of the mantle clock echoed softly in the background.

"You really believe that, don't you, Grandma?"

"Yes, with all my heart."

Cradling his hand in hers, Grandma redirected the conversation. "Let's put these dishes in the sink and then get back to the original question you asked, okay?"

"Sounds good to me," the boy added as he got up from his chair.

A. J. was eager to get to the heart of the matter as he pulled his chair up to the stately oak table. The glowing chandelier illuminated the Bibles.

"Now we're going to finally crack open that question that started your search, A. J."

"It took us a while, didn't it?" A. J. replied. "But it was worth the journey. I'm learning more than I ever thought I would."

"Good. I know you still have some lingering questions about the power of Jesus. But listen to what the authorities who opposed Jesus said about him."

A. J. leaned back, clasping his hands behind his neck, ready to absorb the new information.

"Well, here, you can read it too," Grandma said while handing him a Bible. "It's in St. Mark, chapter three, verse eleven. Do you want to read it?"

"No. Go ahead."

Grandma cleared her throat while they both found the reference. "And the scribes which came down from Jerusalem said, 'He hath Beelzebub,' and by the prince of the devils casteth he out devils.'"

A. J. nearly came out of his chair. "Beelzebub! Who's that?"

"That was a name they used for the one who was, well, the prince of the devils."

"Let me get this straight now," A. J. interrupted. "They were saying that Jesus had the prince of the devils with Him or in Him, and this is why He was able to cast devils out of others?"

"Yes."

Grandma allowed him to study that thought for a while. Then she asked another question. "What else do you notice about that passage?"

"Well, let's see now. I hardly know what to say."

"Let me put it another way. Who are the characters mentioned in that verse?"

"Well, there are the scribes that came down from Jerusalem. I assume they were the religious leaders of that day." A. J. replied.

"That's correct. Who else is mentioned?"

"Uh, Beelzebub. And you say he was the prince of the devils, right?"

"That too is correct."

A. J. continued studying the passage without commenting. Grandma nudged him further.

"Who else is mentioned in that verse?"

"There are no other names here."

"What about the pronoun *he?* Who does that refer to?"

After reading the verse quietly, A. J. faced his grandmother.

"I guess that would be Jesus."

"Yes, that's right. So now we have identified three different characters: the religious leaders, the prince of the devils, and Jesus. Look closely. What is this incident really telling us?"

"Well, like I said, the scribes were accusing Jesus of using the power of the devil to cast out devils."

"There's still something here, A. J., which I'm not sure you understand. By saying what they did, what are the scribes admitting about Jesus?"

The light suddenly went on after A. J. studied the passage again. "Of course! Now I see it! They are admitting that Jesus really did cast out devils."

"Does that answer your question, then? I mean, if the opponents of Jesus didn't dispute the fact that he cast out devils, surely we can believe that he had this power."

"You're right. Yes, you're right."

"Okay, now we need to address the other part of this verse, the part that says he used the power of the devil to do that."

"I've been thinking about this while we were discussing the other parts. Why would the devil cast out himself? It doesn't make sense."

"Oh, you are so right. Go ahead and read the next four verses."

A. J. read the next four verses with a new boldness.

"'And he called them unto him, and said unto them in parables, 'How can Satan cast out Satan? And if a kingdom be divided against itself, that kingdom cannot stand. And if a house be divided against itself, that house cannot stand. And if Satan rise up against himself, and be divided, he cannot stand, but hath an end.'""

The young man reread the passage silently a couple times before responding again.

"Wow! What an answer!"

"Jesus always seemed to have the right thoughts and words at the right time," Grandma interjected. "He had a way of simplifying very difficult concepts so that anyone could understand."

"I'll bet those leaders were, like, shell-shocked. They probably thought they were going to convince the people that Jesus was a fake. Instead, it looks like he turned the tables on them."

"I figured you would be able to grasp what was happening there. By the way, A. J., you never did tell me why you were so interested in this passage."

"Oh, I didn't, did I?"

With that, A. J. recounted in detail all that happened with the quote of Lincoln he discovered in the courthouse.

"So you see," he said as he was finishing, "I couldn't understand why a political person like Lincoln would be using the same quotation put forth by Jesus, a spiritual leader. But, you know, I think I'm beginning to see a connection between the two situations. Yes, I think I'm beginning to see."

AN UNTURNED STONE

A. J. entered his senior year with an optimistic attitude. He was determined to make the best of his final year. His classmates recognized it immediately. The teachers were pleasantly surprised.

American History II soon proved to be A. J.'s favorite subject. An advanced history course offered by Bridges Community High School, it focused upon the rich heritage of Virginia and West Virginia. Mr. Harnel, in his seventh year at Bridges, led lively discussions and directed research highlighting Virginia's role in the early development of the United States.

Mr. Harnel, in particular, had noticed a sparkle of enthusiasm that A. J. had not shown previously in high school. He stopped him in the hall on the third day of school.

"A. J., I'm going to assign an oral report to be given by each student after the first three weeks of class. With only twelve students enrolled this semester, we should have time for an in-depth discussion from each one. Which topic would you like?"

"I'm kind of partial to the Civil War era, especially General Robert E. Lee. Do you think I could do something pertaining to him?"

"Oh, sure," he replied. "The only thing is, however, that is a pretty broad topic. Could you narrow it down to something more specific about General Lee?

"I think I could. I'll need a little time to think about it."

"Try to come up with something by the day after tomorrow, okay?"

"Sure thing. I'll be ready."

"I've heard some very positive comments, Grandma, from the teachers about A. J.'s attitude this fall. Even his classmates are commenting to the teachers," Judge Evans reported to Grandma.

"Really?"

"Yes, I have. And did you see that article in the paper about Robert E. Lee?"

"I did. I enjoyed reading it."

"So did I. You know, Grandma, Mr. Harnel would not have submitted it to the paper unless he thought it really had merit."

"I'm very grateful, Judge. God is performing a miracle in the boy's life. It's simply amazing."

"I've seen a definite change in his outlook. He does have something troubling him, however."

"Oh, really," Grandma said. "What's that?"

"He is still haunted by that incident at the cemetery. It eats at him all the time. He can't get over it, why someone would visit his mother's grave and then take off running like he did. It's like … like someone is violating the one thing he holds sacred."

"It does seem awfully strange," Grandma responded. "And kind of scary too. What about the flowers? Do you think there is any connection there at all?"

"I've been wondering the same thing. And if the flowers are fresh, where would the person get them?"

The two faced each other. Judge Evans slowly raised his eyebrows.

"I've got a hunch, Grandma, that maybe those flowers were purchased here in town. Do you think you could conduct a little private investigation into that?"

"Well, I guess I could. Just what do you have in mind?"

"It's just a hunch, my dear, just a hunch. We'll see if it works out."

"Good morning, Irene," Mrs. Wilken said cheerily as she entered the town's only floral shop. "My, it smells good in here."

"Oh, thank you, and good morning to you, Grandma. It's a pleasant surprise to see you today. What brings you in?"

"I'm having some company tomorrow evening. Just thought I'd splurge a little."

"That's nice. I'm glad you thought of me."

"How is business, Irene? I know some places are slowing down a bit."

"Oh, we're keeping fairly steady. The usual local traffic, the homecoming game coming up this weekend, and now and then an out-of-town visitor. You know how it goes."

"I'm glad to hear that, Irene. It's always good to see our local businesses doing well. What have you got that would brighten a dining table?"

"Well, it depends on your taste. Over here are some beautiful—at least I think they're beautiful—artificial arrangements that I put together."

"They are beautiful, but, no, I don't think I want anything artificial. I want something that's going to be vibrant, possibly aromatic. It doesn't have to be anything that lasts for a long time."

"Well, in that case, you probably want a fresh flower arrangement."

"Yes, that's exactly what I need, but I didn't know whether or not you kept fresh flowers around for something like this."

"I do now."

"Oh, really?"

"Well, it's not a huge demand," Irene said as she led Grandma to the back of the shop. "It's the strangest thing, though. A fella from out-of-town somewhere comes in about once every month asking for a fresh flower arrangement."

"Do you recognize the man?"

"No. I've never seen him in my life."

"Huh," Mrs. Wilken tried not to seem too interested. "Did he leave a name or an indication where he is from?"

"No. He always pays by cash and doesn't stick around too long."

Irene picked up a few roses with some green ivy and carnations. "Would something like this be suitable?"

"That would be great," Grandma replied. "If maybe you could find one more type of flower to go with that, I think it would look great and be fairly fragrant. I'll trust your judgment."

"When would you like it?"

"Could you have it by noon tomorrow?"

"Noon tomorrow it is. Thanks so much for your order."

"You're most welcome. We're sure happy to have your business in town. Oh, Irene, one more thing. You've got my curiosity aroused about this stranger. Has he been coming long?"

"Well, let's see. I think about four months now. It seems he always comes near the end of the month. I'd be expecting him about any day now. I don't ask many questions because he doesn't appear to want to offer any information, and I sure don't want to drive him away. You know what I mean, don't you?"

"Certainly. Well, thank you very much. See you tomorrow about noon."

"Generally, I wouldn't care about who shops in our town, Grandma." Judge Evans scratched his head before continuing. "But in this case, I think we have reasons enough to want to know more about this man. If we don't find out, it could be detrimental to your grandson."

"I hope it's not detrimental to him if we *do* find out."

71

The judge shot a quizzical look at the older woman.

"Sounds like you have something running through your mind, right?"

"Just a hunch, Judge, just a hunch. We'll see how it pans out."

He chuckled while giving her a tender embrace.

"Thanks for your investigative work, Grandma. By the way, who are your guests that are going to enjoy that fresh flower arrangement?"

"Haven't you heard? I figure it's about time I pay back some of my very dear friends for all the help they have given to me and my family. I hope they can come."

"Well, who are they?"

"I thought maybe you and your wife, along with Doc and his wife, would join me for a soup buffet, green salad, and cinnamon roll get-together. Are you free?"

"Let us bring the green salad and it's a date."

"Perfect. I'll call Doc and see if they will be available. See you all at five thirty tomorrow evening?"

"It would take a lot to keep us away from your soup extravaganza. Thanks for the invite. We'll be there."

"Grandma, your continual energy amazes me," Ruth Evans commented as everyone finished the meal. The judge's beautiful wife then asked the older lady, "How do you keep your youthful vitality?"

"I must use what the Lord has given," Grandma replied. "He will have me give an account for it someday. Besides, this type of evening seems to give me added energy."

"Oh, don't tell me," Doc chimed in. "We're liable to be up past midnight if that's the case."

As the laughter subsided, Grandma reached out to the two sitting nearest her, the judge on her left and Kathryn Roberts on her right. As she started talking, everyone around the table followed her lead and took the hand of their neighbor.

"I don't know what I would have done without the four of you these last four years. God be praised; you have given me so much strength. Thank you so much."

Doc Roberts said, "The thanks go to you, Grandma. You have blazed a trail of goodness for us to follow."

Together, they recited the Lord's Prayer.

Filling the silence following the prayer, Ruth Evans commented, "Your flowers look nice, Grandma. Where did you get them?"

"Right here in town at Irene's floral shop."

"Did you have to special order them? I didn't know she kept flowers like that."

"You're right. I don't think she kept a lot of fresh flowers on hand in the past. Lately, however, she has had a visitor coming in about once a month to purchase a nice bouquet."

Quietness enveloped the cozy dining room. Finally, Mrs. Roberts echoed everyone's thoughts.

"That is strange. Do you think that has anything to do with the mysterious appearance of flowers on your daughter's grave, Grandma?"

"Well," Grandma sighed, "it does seem a bit more than coincidental."

"Yes, Kathryn, I do think there is a connection," Judge Evans added. "And I think it's up to the five of us here to connect the dots."

"How are we going to do that?" asked Mrs. Evans.

"Well, what's the date today?" Judge Evans asked.

Doc Roberts checked the calendar.

"It's September nineteenth."

"Okay. Remember, Grandma, how Irene said the stranger always came toward the end of the month? I'm thinking he'll make his visit during the next five days."

"You sound pretty sure of yourself, Judge," Grandma prodded. "What makes you think you are right?"

"Still playing my hunches, Grandma. Do you think we can take Irene into our confidence? It would be nice to have someone tip us off when he shows up."

Grandma thought about it. Before she could answer, Mrs. Roberts spoke.

"I think you can rest assured your secret is safe with her. She is not a gossip."

"I agree," added Grandma. "If she knows how important this is, I'm sure she will cooperate."

"Good. We'll ask her to call you when the man enters her shop. While he's looking around, maybe she can think of some reason to speak to you. Then we can put our plan into action."

"What's our plan? Should we just kind of unexpectedly show up at the floral shop and talk with him?"

"No, we can't do that," the judge responded. "We need to wait until he actually takes the flowers to the cemetery."

"Won't he have a chance of getting away on us, just like he did when A. J. was there?" Kathryn asked.

"Well, A. J. told us that the man he encountered left by way of the back side of the cemetery. I'm thinking that after he gets the flowers, he will park along Birdsong Avenue on the other side of the hill and then enter from the back side."

"That does make sense," Doc said. "He will try to leave himself a way out."

The judge continued.

"Here's what I'm thinking. Some of us will wait inside the church. When he gets to Loretta's grave, or a little bit before, we will start walking through the cemetery like we are just visiting. Hopefully, we will be able to strike up a conversation with him. All we want to do is talk to him and find out what is going on."

"Don't you think he will get suspicious and maybe a little frightened?" Ruth wondered.

"I don't think so. After all, it's not really unusual for older people to leisurely stroll through a cemetery. Maybe we can even have flower arrangements or something in our hands to place on different graves."

"That would probably be a good idea," Ruth responded.

"But in case he does get frightened, we will have a backup plan. Two of us will have followed him at a distance in our car. When he has walked over the hill, we will pull the car up behind his."

"Then if he does do the same thing he did with A. J., he'll find a surprise, right?" said Grandma.

"That's right. It will be a little more uncomfortable, but at least we might be able to talk with him."

"Sounds like you've given this quite a bit of thought, dear," Mrs. Evans said.

"I just think it's important we find out what is happening here. If anyone has anything to add or changes to make to this, feel free to say it."

"No, I think this has been well thought out," interjected Doc. "And I think that only one man should be waiting at the church. I suggest that you, Ruth, and Grandma be waiting at the church. Kathryn and I will bring the backup car. To me, that makes the most sense and will be less threatening to our visitor."

Everyone nodded in agreement.

"Okay," Judge said. "Let's finalize our plans and make sure our communication system is in order. I'll talk to Irene tomorrow."

The plan worked beautifully. As expected, the stranger did show up within the five-day period. The calling wheel began, and soon, everyone was in place. When the visitor approached Loretta's grave with the flowers, he noticed three interested townspeople also walking in the cemetery. At first he appeared startled and turned to leave, but then he seemed to think better of it.

"Wonderful time of the year, isn't it?" Judge Evans quipped nonchalantly as he neared Loretta's resting place. "The air is so crisp and inviting, it makes a person feel like he could do about anything."

Glancing up, the stranger acknowledged the remarks with a smile and a nod of his head.

Wayne Drayer

The ladies had veered off in a different direction, placing wreaths at various sites.

"I see you have remembered Mrs. Franklin with flowers." Judge Evans waited for a response, but none was forthcoming. "Well, she deserves it. What a fine lady she was! One of the best our town has ever seen."

The younger man, who appeared to be in his late forties, remained silent. He began to shuffle his feet nervously, apparently eager to be on his way. Experience, however, was on Judge Evan's side as he continued the conversation.

"Did you know her? Oh, I'm sorry. That's an unfair question. Of course you knew her, or you wouldn't be here."

Again, a few seconds of silence followed before he answered. "Yes, I knew her. She meant a lot to me too."

"If you've got a second, I'd like you to meet someone." The judge turned to the ladies and called, "Grandma, would you come over here? I'd like you to meet this young man." He turned back to the stranger. "She's really not my grandma. That's just what everyone in town calls her."

The visitor chuckled appreciatively, responding, "She looks like a warm person that everyone would like to have as a grandma."

"You've got that right. The lady walking with Grandma is my wife, Ruth."

A slight breeze stirred as the ladies approached.

"Ladies, I want you to meet a young man who knew Loretta. What did you say your name was, sir?"

"I guess I didn't tell you my name."

"Wow, that's a relief. I was thinking maybe I forgot it already."

"My name is Ed, Ed Greene."

Grandma reached her hand toward him.

"Glad to meet you, Mr. Greene. I'm sorry, but I guess I don't remember ever meeting you. Of course, I am getting older and my forgetter's getting better."

76

Turning to the visitor, the judge intervened. "Loretta was Grandma's daughter."

A stunned silence wedged into the group. The visitor stared at the ground a few seconds, regained his composure, and faced Grandma.

"I didn't expect you to know me. I didn't really know Loretta. My name isn't Ed Greene, either."

"Oh?" Grandma responded. "Would you mind telling us your real name?"

"My name …" the visitor answered slowly. "My name is Hank Bensely."

Grandma raised her hands to her mouth to stifle an audible gasp. Anyone who had attended the trial following Loretta's death would recognize that name.

"But, you're not—"

"No, I'm not the one who was driving the car. That was my brother, Jacob."

A few leaves that had fallen early danced around the feet of the quartet, stirred by a cool September breeze. In the distance, the faint blare of the morning train passing through Bridges could be heard. A neighbor's barking dog punctuated the stillness. The four people standing near Loretta's gravesite exchanged timid glances, at a loss for words.

Judge Evans took the initiative.

"I guess you're doing this out of respect for Loretta?"

"Yes, out of respect for her, and at the request of my brother."

"He asked you to do this? Why?" Grandma wanted to know.

"He's in the fourth year of his seven-year prison term. Not a day has gone by that he hasn't been tortured by the events of that tragic weekend. Especially after reading and hearing about the type of woman she was and how much grief it has brought to her family."

"How did he hear of all that, I mean, being so far away?" asked Mrs. Evans.

"Oh, word gets around."

"A lot of time has gone by," interrupted Judge Evans. "Why is this happening at this time?"

"It's a long story."

"We have plenty of time. Nothing is pushing us. There are a few benches under those trees over there. Let's make ourselves comfortable."

The group looked up just in time to see Doc Roberts and his wife coming over the hill. The visitor was taken aback when he saw them all waving to each other but quickly figured it out.

"Looks like you had staked me out pretty well."

"We just wanted to make sure we would be able to talk to you," the judge replied. "We had earlier reports from a youngster about a man who liked to exit over the back hill."

"Oh yes," Hank replied. "I remember."

The benches were arranged so six people could sit comfortably. Mr. Evans kindly introduced Doc and his wife and informed them of what had taken place. He turned his attention to Hank and invited him to continue.

"My brother has always been a very kind and considerate person. He was not an alcoholic. Drinking was never a problem for him. Oh, maybe he'd have a drink now and then, but he was always in control. The bottle was not his master, but it occasionally became his crutch. Obviously, one time it did become his master, and it ended in disaster."

"That's truly unfortunate. What led to that?" the judge asked.

"About six years ago, Jacob and his family met with some serious misfortunes. Family ties began to unravel. A couple years passed by until he came home one evening and was greeted by the news that his wife had left him. That Friday evening he turned to the bottle for consolation."

Grandma kept her head down while drying her eyes.

"I'm sorry, ma'am, to drag you through this again."

"It is difficult, but don't worry about me. We want to hear your story."

"Well, like I said, the events of that tragedy have haunted my brother every day. About a year ago, he became interested in and then became part of a Bible study group. Pastors and other Bible scholars would visit the prison on a regular basis, and soon there was a fairly sizeable group of interested prisoners."

"I've heard a lot about prison ministry efforts," said Doc. "I've often wondered how effective they were."

"I can't vouch for other prisoners, but it has worked wonders for my brother. I've known him all my life, and I know when he is being genuine. He began reading the scriptures avidly on his own. About six months ago, well he made a huge change in his life."

Grandma's sober mood brightened like the sun escaping a cloud. "So you could really see a difference in him?"

"Oh, most definitely. Don't ask me to explain it, though. His whole outlook seemed different. He still carried a weight about the accident, but he definitely made his peace with God."

"And the flowers?" Kathryn asked.

"That's when he asked me if I would place a bouquet of fresh flowers on Loretta's grave each month, on the date of the accident if possible."

"I'm glad he was able to find peace in his life," Grandma added.

"Thank you. I am too. But he is still searching for something."

"What's that?" Doc asked.

"He's found his peace with God. Now he wants to find peace with Loretta's family."

Judge Evans searched Grandma's face and then turned back to Hank.

"Do you remember the young man you encountered here before you escaped over the hill?"

"Yes. That was rather frightening to me. He appeared very distraught."

"He was. To him, his mother's grave has been a very sacred place. He couldn't understand why a stranger would be near it."

Again, it took a few moments for the visitor to recover before he spoke.

"Would he understand if he knew everything I just told you?"

The judge pondered the suggestion a moment.

"I don't know," he said. "I don't know."

Grandma came to the rescue.

"I can't begin to tell you what A. J.—that's his name—has gone through since the accident. It's affected him, I think, more than anyone. He made great strides this past summer and is just beginning to find himself again. He's wondering about the flowers, how they got there. How he will take this latest bit of news, well, I don't know. I just don't know. How will he react to this news? It will be interesting, to say the least."

"I'm afraid it's going to set him back—how far I don't know—but I don't like it at all." Grandma hesitated and then spoke again. "I'm getting too old to go through another crisis like this."

"Maybe he's mature enough now, strong enough, to handle it in stride," Doc Roberts offered.

"I wish I could believe that. With all my heart, I hope you're right. But I know how protective he has been with anything involving his mother. It just seems to me he will look at this as an intrusion of his privacy."

"Tell me again, will you, what the letter said, Grandma," Judge Evans spoke quietly and slowly.

"It's from Hank. Of course, he always keeps in close touch with his brother. He shared with him everything that happened, you know, meeting us and all that we talked about. He knows about A. J. and that the boy seems to have the toughest time dealing with the accident. He would like to meet us. His main goal is to make peace with us."

While the three of them looked blankly at each other, pondering the situation, the door to the restaurant opened. Their faces brightened when they recognized Joe. He seemed to be looking for someone. Catching his eye, they waved for him to come to their table.

"Well, this is a pleasant surprise," Grandma said. "I didn't know you weren't working today."

"Things have started to slow down a bit at the plant. For the next few weeks, we're taking every Friday off until demand begins to pick up, hopefully later this fall. I'm not interfering, am I?"

"Certainly not," said Doc. "We're glad to have you with us."

"I tried calling you earlier, Mom. When you didn't answer, I took a chance that you might be here."

"I'm glad you found me. What's on your mind?"

"I thought maybe we could begin making plans for that open house at Jessie's school. That's only a week from tomorrow, you know."

"Yes, that is coming right up. I've got it on my calendar. Is A. J. still looking forward to it?"

"Oh, yes. He's very excited. He's keeping so busy, though, that he hasn't had much time to think about it. Jessie called last night to remind us."

Grandma looked down to stir her coffee.

"Joe, there's something very important that has happened recently. We were just now discussing it, trying to decide the best course of action to take."

"Oh, I hope I'm not intruding."

"Not at all. We would have spoken to you soon about it. It looks like now is the best time."

"Well, I do have some extra time right now. I just want to be home before five."

Grandma began speaking slowly while placing her hand on Joe's.

"We know who has been placing flowers on Loretta's grave."

Joe continued to look intently at the others, waiting for Mrs. Wilken to continue. Slowly, she pronounced his name.

"It's Hank Bensely."

Joe's body unconsciously twitched at the sound of the last name. He sat up straighter as he spoke to the trio of friends.

"Hank Bensely? But, but that's not—"

"No," Judge Evans interrupted, "that's not the man who was driving the car. It's his brother. Jacob is still in prison, serving the fourth year of a seven-year term."

"But … but, why? Why the flowers?"

Grandma reached over and touched Joe's open hands.

"It seems Jacob has come to terms with himself—and with God. His brother says that Jacob has found peace with God. Now he's trying to reach out to find peace with Loretta's family."

Joe looked helplessly at the others.

"So he's having his brother place fresh flowers on Loretta's grave as a token of reconciliation?"

"Every month," Doc answered, "on the day corresponding to the date of the accident."

Judge Evans signaled the waitress to refill the coffee cups. It provided a nice break for each to ponder the situation. With fresh coffee steaming, Grandma continued the conversation.

"Now, Joe, something new has developed."

Quizzically, he looked at Grandma.

"Jacob would like to meet with the four of us. I guess he's pretty serious about wanting to make peace."

"He wants to meet with the four of us?" he whispered.

"No, no," Grandma replied. "He wants to meet with you, Jessie, A. J., and me."

"Oh, oh," Joe said with a chuckle. "No, I don't think so. You and me, sure, that might be okay. Jessie? Well, maybe. But A. J.? No, I don't think so."

"That's what I was thinking too, Joe." She looked at all of them around the table as she talked. "I mean, A. J. has come a long way this year, but I don't think he is ready to deal with something like this."

"You're probably right, Grandma," Judge Evans interjected. "But maybe he could be coached into handling this correctly. He definitely has matured. What we need, though, is time."

"I'd hate to say anything to him right now," Joe responded. "He told me this morning that Mr. Harnel asked him to consider giving the senior speech at the Veterans Day commemoration next month. I think he is planning to talk to you about it, Grandma."

"Well, that's good," said the judge. "It sounds like a great opportunity for A. J., and it will give us time to plan a strategy. What do you think, Doc?"

"Sounds reasonable to me. However, I wouldn't want Jacob to think he is being blown off. Do you think you could explain the situation to Hank, Grandma? Tell him you won't be able to meet with him until at least December. Feel free to explain why if he asks."

"I think I could do that. I think he'll understand too, if we level with him," Grandma replied.

A. J. planned to talk with Judge Evans before he spoke with Grandma about the upcoming Veterans Day celebration. Before going up the steps to the courthouse, he glanced across the street just in time to see the four conversationalists emerge from the restaurant. Instinctively, he called out to them and waved.

"Uh-oh," said Grandma as she waved back. "I think our plans are changing. What do we do now?"

"I don't think we have much choice," drawled Doc. "He'll know if we're trying to fake anything."

"Yes, you're right," the judge replied. "Let's invite him to join us in my office. Do you still have to be home by five, Joe?"

"Well, no. Not if A. J. isn't there."

"Okay. Let's all go up to my office, then—and face the music."

The first part of the conversation went about as expected. The adults, without making it obvious, watched A. J.'s facial expressions to see how everything was going down.

"Now, wait a minute. Let me get this straight," A. J. said after listening a few minutes. "You're telling me that the man putting flowers on my mother's grave is a brother to the man that ..." A. J.'s voice trailed off while his gaze was directed nowhere.

"I know it might sound a little strange, A. J., but—"

"Strange?" A. J. loudly echoed. "Why did he run when I came?"

"I'm sure he didn't know who you were," added Doc. "Actually, he was doing it for his brother, who is still in prison."

"Oh," A. J. responded flippantly. "So now a few flowers are supposed to make us forget all about the past, as though nothing ever happened? Is that what he's trying to do?"

"Well, no, not exactly. We all know it's not that easy." The judge paused a few moments and then continued. "He really wants to do more."

"More?" A. J.'s contorted facial expression sent a chill through Grandma. She reached over to rub his hand. Gently, she answered his question.

"He would like to find peace with us."

"I ... I don't understand. What's going on?"

"Give us a chance to tell you all that has happened, son. It might make things a little more clear."

With that, the adults rehearsed the happenings of recent days, while A. J. received each revelation with unbridled curiosity. When they were finished, they waited for A. J. to respond. The lad cleared his throat before softly speaking.

"I had come here this afternoon, Judge, to tell you and then the others that I was planning to give the talk at our annual Veterans Day celebration. I was really excited about it when Mr. Harnel asked if I would give the speech. But now, with all of this coming up, I don't know if I have the heart to do it anymore."

"If it would help, we could wait until after the Veterans Day weekend," Grandma offered.

"That would just be like an iron yoke around my neck," A. J. replied. "It would ruin the weekend."

No one spoke. The meeting abruptly ended after A. J. spoke again.

"You know, things were looking pretty good. We had the open house scheduled at Jessie's school. Then we had the Veterans Day celebration coming up. Now, this throws a wrench into everything. I don't know if I even want to meet with him. I need time to think about it."

Everyone was silent, looking at the floor or exchanging blank stares with each other.

"Can I have a ride home, Dad?"

CLOUDY STREAM

"I didn't sleep well last night," A. J. nonchalantly told his dad while pouring orange juice.

"Neither did I," Joe replied absentmindedly.

"So what are your thoughts about it now, Dad? I mean, you know, you'd think the guy would at least have the decency to leave us alone."

"Yeah, I know what you mean. From what I've been told, though, I don't think he's just trying to hassle us."

"I was doing just fine without him in my life. I've been trying to block out any memory of him."

"Well, A. J., maybe that's not the best thing to do."

"I know, I know. I've been giving some thought to what you said last night about giving him a chance."

"Go on," Joe said after an interval of silence.

"I don't see why we should give him a chance. My mother didn't get another chance, did she?"

"Of course you're right, son. But, sometime, we've got to let go of that, don't you agree?"

"Sometime, maybe. But it's going to be on my own terms—not because a criminal wants me to."

Joe struggled enough within himself, so he didn't feel like preaching. He dropped the conversation, hoping A. J. would also take the hint.

"Like I said," A. J. continued, "I don't think he deserves a chance to talk about whatever is on his mind. But neither do I want him to ruin any more of my life."

"I don't follow your reasoning."

"He sure threw a boulder into my life for years. Now that things are beginning to look up a little, he shows up again. I really don't want to talk to him. But if that's the only way to get rid of him, maybe that's the thing we have to do."

A long silence followed while each continued eating breakfast. Just as A. J. was preparing to get up from the table, his father spoke.

"I agree with some of your feelings, but not all."

"Oh?" A. J. said without getting up.

"I'm not anxious to meet with him, either. However, I think we should give him the benefit of trying to come to a wholesome peace."

A. J. slowly raised himself from the chair. Joe took note of his son's six-foot, two-inch muscular frame that nearly filled the doorway leading to the living room. He marveled at the change in his son over the past eighteen months.

"I wish I could be as optimistic about this as you are, Dad. I'll go along with whatever you think is best."

"I appreciate your willingness, son. When would you like to go?"

"For me, the sooner the better. I'd like to get it out of the way before the Veterans Day celebration."

"I'll try to talk with Grandma and the others today."

"Okay. I'll be at the library. It's open till four on Saturdays. I need to keep working on that speech."

"Leaving at six o'clock was a good idea, Joe. Jessie would have been disappointed if we couldn't eat lunch with her."

"That's what I was thinking too, Grandma," Joe replied. "We should have plenty of time to stop soon for a cup of coffee or a Coke."

"Sounds good to me," A. J. laughingly added from the backseat. "Getting up at five kind of jolted my system."

"I thought you've been rather quiet back there," teased Grandma. "Pretty tired, huh?"

"Well, I'm a little tired, yeah. But mainly I'm just kind of anxious about the whole weekend. I'm not sure what to expect."

"None of us are," Grandma said hesitatingly. "I guess we'll just kind of have to roll with the punches."

"I don't know how good I'll be at that. This was supposed to be a great weekend. You know, getting to see Jessie's college for the first time and meeting her friends and all that. Now this other thing, like having a root canal done, waits to ruin everything."

Joe peered through the rearview mirror. "It's the best we could do, son."

"I know," the youngster quipped. "But I almost wish we could have gone to the prison first, just to get that out of the way. I probably won't be able to enjoy the open house because of that dark cloud waiting for me."

"This is the only way it would work, A. J.," Grandma consoled. "Jessie's roommate's family is going to take her back to the college after our visit at the prison. They couldn't meet us yesterday or today because of getting ready for the open house."

Five minutes of driving in silence seemed a lot longer. Joe tried to concentrate on the road ahead. Grandma contemplated the situation, wishing things were different. A. J. broke the silence.

"I can almost read your mind, Grandma. You think I should be more mature about this whole thing."

"It's not that I think you're immature. Goodness, you've made a lot of progress in four years. I only wish that ... well, I guess I wish you would look at it more from his situation."

"I hear what you're saying. But I think you need to remember I was the one in that car with Mom when it rolled over and over and didn't seem to want to stop."

Again, no one spoke for a while until A. J. spoke again.

"There was a time I kept blaming myself for what happened. Finally, when I was able to mentally climb out of that ravine, things began to change for the better—"

"We were so glad to see that happen," Grandma interrupted, beaming as she turned her head as far as she could toward the back. "I can tell you a lot of people were concerned, and many were praying for you."

"I know they were. I guess I owe a lot of gratitude to a lot of people. That's one reason I agreed to talk at the Veterans Day celebration. Kind of give back to the community for what they've done. It's kind of strange too. The more I think about it and prepare myself, the more excitement I feel about presenting it."

"Well, I must say your enthusiasm is making me anxious to hear it. You're putting a lot of work into it."

Try as she might, however, Grandma couldn't keep the conversation steered away from the old memories.

"You know, the more I extricated myself from being the cause of the accident, the more blame I piled onto the driver of the other car," A. J. continued.

Joe had remained quiet for a long time. Now he spoke just a single word. "Forgiveness."

"What?" A. J. asked.

"Forgiveness."

"That's what I thought you said. And?"

"That's the only way we're going to make it through this thing. It's the only true antidote for bitter feelings."

"Bitter! Who's bitter?"

The ensuing silence surrounding A. J.'s words echoed with a hollow ring.

"Well," he said softly, almost ashamedly, "*bitter* sounds kind of harsh. I don't think I hold that kind of resentment."

Keeping his eyes straight ahead, Joe weighed his words carefully. "But you're still not willing to give him a chance."

"We're going there Monday, aren't we?" A. J. retorted.

89

"Yes, we are," Joe responded resignedly. "But it seems to me your mind is already made up. All I'm asking is that you go in with an open mind."

A sign for a nearby diner rescued the trio from any further disagreements. Grandma was the first to notice it.

"Oh, look, there's a restaurant only a mile off the highway. Anyone else ready for a midmorning break?"

"I sure am. Driving is tiring me. A. J., would you like to drive the last hundred miles when we finish here?"

"Sounds good to me. I'm getting a little cramped back here."

PART THREE

---

*The congress of the United States recommends and
approves the Holy Bible for use in all schools.*
—Resolution voted by Congress
1782

*What is taught in the schools in one generation
will be the government of the next.*
—Abraham Lincoln

*I shall be telling this with a sigh,
many ages and ages hence;
Two roads diverged in a wood, and I—I
took the one less traveled by,
And that has made all the difference.*
—Robert Frost

CLEANSING WATERS

"That was a super lunch. All I need now is a place to stretch out and relax." Joe looked around to see if anyone agreed with him.

"Sounds good to me," Grandma joined in. "What time does the evening program begin, Jessie?"

"We're going to meet at the chapel about four o'clock. From there we will walk together to Alumni Hall, where we plan to eat about five o'clock. Then at seven, President VanCortland will officially welcome everyone."

"Isn't he your roommate's father?"

"Yes, he is, Grandma. I was fortunate to get Sharon as a roommate. They are a wonderful family."

"I'm surprised she doesn't live at home with her parents."

"It's part of the rules, Dad. They feel students will assume responsibility quicker if they're not living at home with their parents. All part of their teaching curriculum."

"When will we get to meet them?" A. J. asked.

"Probably when we all meet at the chapel this afternoon. They're busy now putting on the finishing touches."

"You mentioned in your letter they also have a son," Grandma said.

"Oh, yes, Thomas the second. He's a sweetheart! We call him Tommy."

"Will he be with us tonight?"

"I don't think so. But we're planning to go see him tomorrow."

"He doesn't live here?" Joe inquired.

"No. Tommy has been physically handicapped since he was twelve. He's soon going to be twenty-six years old. It has become too big of a task for Sharon's parents to care for him. He lives in a home for the disabled about twelve miles from here."

"What kinds of problems does he have?" A. J. asked thoughtfully.

"He was injured in a swimming accident. While playing with a group of his buddies, one of his friends thoughtlessly pushed him when he was off-balance. He hit the side of the pool, leaving him paralyzed from his waist down."

"Will we get to meet him while we're here?" A. J. asked.

"Oh, yes. I'm sure they've scheduled that in our agenda."

"Well," Grandma interrupted, "we will be meeting everyone in a few hours. I'd like to relax awhile and then freshen up a bit."

"I've got the perfect place for you. With Sharon busy at the school, there's room in my apartment."

"I'm not tired. I'd just as soon do a little exploring," A. J. said.

"Okay, A. J. I'll take Dad and Grandma to my apartment. Then I'll come back and give you a little pretour of the campus. Unless you'd like to come see the apartment now."

"No. I'll just wander around this general area and wait for you."

Jessie was on top of her game when she returned to A. J.

"Let's go first to the Biology Studies building. That's where I spend most of my time since I switched to premed."

"Premed? Wow! When did you switch to that?"

"About two years ago. You may have forgotten that I told you."

"Yeah, I suppose I did. I was pretty preoccupied with myself then. Wasn't paying much attention to anything."

"You've changed a lot this past year, A. J. I mean, for the good. I'm glad you came this weekend."

"It's great being here. I think I could get attached to this place."

"They would love to have you here. I've been telling them about you."

A. J. aimlessly kicked a small stone, sending it rolling on the sidewalk leading across campus.

"What do you think about Monday, Jess?"

"You mean, when we go to the prison to visit—"

"Yeah. Are you looking forward to it?"

"Well, I'm not actually looking forward to it, but I'm not dreading it, either."

"It doesn't bother you, then?"

"Not really. I'd rather stay away, but I'm kind of anxious to see what effect four years of prison has had on the man. It sounds like he is searching. I like to think I'm ready to help."

"I'm not there yet, Jess. Don't know if I ever will be."

"A. J., you've come so far. Don't let this stand in your way."

The sister-brother duo walked in silence a couple minutes before Jessie spoke again.

"You know, if there's one thing I've learned while I've been here, it's that there comes a time when we need to try to let go of old hurts."

"I don't know if I can do that, Sis."

"I know. It's hard to do."

"I don't even know if I would know how to let go if I wanted to."

Jessie looked calmly into her brother's eyes.

"The first step is forgiveness."

"Oh, right, forgiveness! Sure, just like that! Forget it ever happened!"

"No, A. J., I didn't say *forget*. We'll never be able to forget what happened."

"Then what do you mean?"

Jessie didn't respond to his excitable question. In a softer voice, he rephrased his thoughts.

"What does it mean to forgive?"

Jessie stared at the sidewalk. Their steps had slowed considerably.

"You know, A. J., for a long time I thought our situation was unique. I looked at our friends, wondering why they didn't have to go through something like we did."

"Did you really, Jess?"

"I sure did."

"You never let on that you felt that way."

"I tried to be strong, so I covered up all my resentment."

"Do you still have those feelings … I mean, it doesn't seem like you do."

"No, I don't. Oh, there are times old feelings try to creep in, but it keeps getting better."

"How were you able to get on top?'

"When I met Tommy."

"Sharon's brother?"

"Yes. When I met him, I thought, here's somebody who knows what it's like to get a raw deal. A friend pushes him and he ends up in a wheelchair for the rest of his life."

"Was he resentful?"

"I think he was in the beginning and maybe for quite a while after that. But by the time I met him, he wasn't. At first I thought he was faking it. The happy attitude, the contented look in his eyes, and all that."

"Was he?"

"No, he is as genuine as a Sunday afternoon chicken dinner."

"How was he able to do that?"

"I finally asked him. He answered one word: forgiveness."

A. J. stood silently with his hands in his pocket. When he didn't respond, Jessie continued.

"When Tommy was able to forgive his friend, he did himself a favor. He freed himself from carrying a grudge, which only drains positive energy."

The boy remained in a solemn, contemplative mood while Jessie continued to present her case.

"A. J., we all saw a huge difference in you when you were finally able to forgive yourself."

The young man looked down at his sister, who was six inches shorter. A hint of tears magnified the blue of her eyes. He wanted to hold her, but she beat him to it. She clasped her hands loosely around the back of his neck.

"Think of the greater strides you could make if you could conquer this next hurdle."

"Jessie," he said hesitatingly, "what you say makes a whole lot of sense. I wish I could, but I just don't think I can."

"You're more than halfway there, A. J., if you really want to. Now you just need to ask for help."

"Ask who?"

"Remember that old saying, 'to err is human but to forgive is …?'" She waited for her brother to finish the sentence.

"Divine … I know."

"That's right. It's not just a catchy saying. It's true. True forgiveness is of God. He will help you forgive."

"But, Jessie, I don't want to say what he did was okay. I can't say that."

"You won't be saying it was okay. We know it wasn't okay for him to do that. He knows it wasn't the right thing to do. We are just saying we will no longer hold him accountable. We leave that in God's hands."

A. J. pulled his hands out of his pockets and placed them around her waist. He drew her close, making sure she could not see his face.

"Jessie, I'm afraid."

"Of what, A. J.?"

"I'm afraid to let go." His voice was soft, then softer. "Afraid that I will dishonor Mom."

Jessie embraced the stillness of the sacred moment.

"Let's suppose, just for a moment, A. J., that Mom knows what we are going through." A slight breeze rustled the fallen leaves while Jessie waited. "What do you think Mom would want us to do?"

Again, he remained silent. She gently pulled herself back and looked into his eyes. "Don't you think she would want us to try to forgive—and get on with our lives?"

"Yes, I suppose you're right, Sis," he said reluctantly. "As many times as she was hurt by others, I never knew her to hold a grudge. Then again, she was just a much better person than I am."

"Let's look at it this way, A. J. What are your options?"

"I don't think I have any," he said.

"Sure, you do."

The young man dropped his arms and sat on a nearby bench. "I know," he said resignedly. "I just don't know if I'm ready to choose."

"By not actively deciding, you are choosing already. And what you have subconsciously chosen is keeping you a slave to your fears."

A. J.'s eyes lit up. "Jessie, you're coming home for the Veterans Day celebration, aren't you?"

"Well, yes, I plan to, but don't change the subject, A. J.!"

"I'm not, Jess. I just had a great idea. How would you like to be part of the platform?"

"You mean—talk that evening? I thought you were giving the speech."

"I am, but it would be great having you there too. You're upbeat and a cool thinker. A few words from you would add so much to the atmosphere. Besides, you were supposed to be the speaker four years ago and got cheated out of it."

"Yes, I remember. But this address is to come from you. By the way, A. J., I've been wondering, what is the theme of your talk?"

"Liberty."

"Liberty? What about liberty?"

"I'm not quite sure yet, but ever since this past summer, especially after reading Mom's letter, the thought of liberty has simply possessed me. I'm just trying to, well, throw a rope around the concept so I can handle it."

"I don't think you'll be able to package it, A. J. It's too big. It's an awesome idea."

"I know. Sometimes, though, I just equate it with freedom. The two words seem to be interchangeable."

"They are, that's true. But if they were exactly the same, there would be no need for two different words, would there?"

"I never thought of it like that before. Well, then, Jess, how do you differentiate between the two?"

"I struggle with a good definition for the two words also. But it's a good struggle, you know? Freedom is probably the most sought after thing in the world today. Our country is built on freedom and liberty."

"See, right there you used both words together, in the same breath."

"I know. They are very much alike. But I think of them a little differently. I guess everyone has their own pet definition."

"What's yours, Sis?"

"You know, A. J., God often uses things we can see to help us understand things we cannot see. So sometimes I combine what I can see in nature with what I read in the scripture to give me a greater comprehension."

"I'm listening."

"You are aware, aren't you, A. J., that liberty and freedom are mentioned often in the Bible?"

"Grandma has pointed it out many times."

"Good. I have memorized one verse that means a lot to me: 'Stand fast, therefore, in the liberty wherewith Christ hath made us free, and be not entangled again with the yoke of bondage.'"

"I like that, Sis. I like the way it uses *liberty*, and *free*, and also *bondage*—the opposite condition—all in one verse!"

"Isn't that super? And notice how it is written: 'in the liberty wherewith Christ has made us free,' or maybe we could say 'in the liberty by which Christ has made us free.' It's almost as if liberty is a vehicle taking us to freedom."

"I kind of see what you mean, Jess."

"It may not be exactly right, but it works for me; then I compare that to a Monarch butterfly."

"You do?"

"Well, it could be any butterfly. I'm just partial to the Monarch. I think of the butterfly life cycle."

"You mean how a caterpillar goes through metamorphosis and becomes a butterfly, right?"

"Exactly. And you know, A. J., every time I study that phenomenon, it seems more unreal than the time before. Think about it; a small caterpillar with just a limited amount of freedom moves about finding food, then at the proper time forms a chrysalis to protect itself, and soon it emerges from the chrysalis changed to a beautiful, magnificent butterfly."

"You sure get excited about that, don't you, Sis?"

"Oh, absolutely, because it's such a universal truth. It can be applied to nations struggling for freedom or to each of us individually facing personal challenges."

"You really should be giving this Veterans Day talk, Jess. This is what it's all about."

"Oh, I think my brother will do just fine," Jessie said with a smile. "You're on the right track." Then, she added thoughtfully, "You know what else I think, A. J.?"

"What?"

"I think this is what Mr. Bensely is seeking—a complete expression of spiritual freedom."

A. J. became quiet and expressionless while fixing his gaze on the sky. Jessie broke the stillness.

"Come on, A. J. We'd better head back to the apartment and get ready for this evening's activities."

"I didn't know you were on the program tonight, Sis," A. J. whispered.

"I wanted it to be a surprise, A. J."

Their conversation was cut short as President VanCortland began speaking.

"Now, to begin our evening, two young ladies have agreed to sing an old favorite for us."

Jessie and Sharon walked to the front of the room. They were a stunning picture standing behind the podium: Jessie, with her blonde hair trailing onto her light-brown dress, and Sharon, whose dark hair contrasted nicely with the yellow dress she wore. Like golden hues of autumn, they presented a beautiful picture to the audience. As lovely as they were in appearance, their voices combined into a rhapsodic harmony delivering "Faith of Our Fathers" as many had never before heard it sung.

When finished, a standing ovation followed them back to their tables. While pulling her chair back for her to be seated, A. J. spoke to Jessie in a low tone.

"I want you to forget about speaking with me at the Veterans Day celebration."

Jessie looked at him, and her smile turned to a troubled expression.

"I want you and Sharon to sing for us that evening."

Her smile returned, along with a look of surprise.

"Are you kidding me?"

"If we can get Sharon's folks to bring her, I'd like nothing better," he whispered.

"Thank you for the beautiful singing, girls. Those of you familiar with the history of our college know the importance of that song to our founding and continuing mission. I'm sure the rest of you will have an opportunity to become familiar with that history during this weekend.

"One of those young ladies is our daughter, Sharon. She is a senior at our school. The other young lady is her roommate, Jessie Franklin. Would you girls stand again while I also introduce Jessie's

101

family, who came all the way from West Virginia to be with us this weekend? Please welcome her brother, A. J., who is considering being with us next fall, her father, and her grandmother."

A warm ovation greeted the visitors.

"I am happy to say that, since our daughter is a roommate to Jessie, we have the inside track on keeping her family at our house the next two nights. Although we are usually a charitable family, I hope no one tempts me by asking to keep them at their house."

A ripple of laughter passed through the audience.

"Following a light evening meal, we will break apart into eight groups. The groups will be allowed to spend twenty minutes with each of the eight different departmental personnel. After the meetings, you are welcome to snack again and enjoy fellowship before we dismiss for the evening."

"Tomorrow morning we will begin our worship service at ten o'clock. Then we will have our big meal for the weekend. About two o'clock, our campus tour will begin. This should last until about four o'clock, at which time our open house will officially end. Feel free to ask any questions as we go along. Thank you very much for coming this weekend."

"When are we going to get to meet Sharon's brother Tommy?" A. J. asked Jessie later that evening.

"She told me that her parents and the rest of us are going to visit him after the campus tours tomorrow. It will be a good way to kind of wind down the weekend. I think you will really like him.

"A. J., were you serious about Sharon and I singing for you at the Veterans Day get-together?" Jessie asked him.

"I couldn't have been more serious. It would be a neat experience. The people would love it."

"Well, then, I'm going to let you in on a little secret. Sharon and I are working on a new song."

"Really? Which one?"

"Not so fast, A. J. We haven't even given it a title yet."

"Haven't given it a title yet? Do you mean you are writing this song?"

"Oh, yes."

"Man, I am learning things I never knew before. I didn't know you two were also songwriters. Can you tell me about it?"

"Not until we're finished. But I think it will fit into your talk very well."

"Jessie, that is super! Now I am getting enthused about that evening."

The eyes of the man on the middle cross transfixed A. J. Absorbed completely by the compassionate, yet painful look, he was oblivious to those around him.

Tommy waited with his family at the back of the room. A. J. and his family had walked to the front of the large activity area to view Tommy's masterpiece, a 36" x 48" painting of the Crucifixion.

The eyes spoke to A. J., as though inviting him into the picture. For a few precious seconds, A. J.'s mind was elevated to heights he had never before experienced. Unexplainably, he felt as one with the suffering Christ.

He could see the scourging whips bearing pieces of bones and metal fragments that had ripped the flesh. He saw blood staining the rocks and ground. He saw the soldiers laughing and cursing as they gambled for a piece of the man's clothing. A few women were weeping and praying. Flashes of lightning lit up the darkening skies and the form of the barely recognizable Savior.

"A. J.? A. J.?"

Jessie's soft voice penetrated the lad's isolation.

"Are you okay?"

"This ... this is so real. I can hardly believe it."

"Tommy didn't exaggerate, A. J.," Grandma whispered. "Look at the words of the prophet Isaiah."

A. J. studied the verses below the painting—words spoken hundreds of years before the Crucifixion:

> He is despised and rejected of men; a man of sorrows, and acquainted with grief: and we hid as it were our faces from him; he was despised and we esteemed him not.
>
> He was wounded for our transgressions, he was bruised for our iniquities: the chastisement of our peace was upon him; and with his stripes we are healed.

"Along the sides are direct quotes of Jesus while on the Cross," his father added. While A. J. looked, the other three each read a quote.

> Father, forgive them; for they know not what they do.
> My God, My God, why hast thou forsaken me?
> It is finished.

Tommy and his family slowly moved up to join the Franklins. Everyone's focus remained on the painting for several minutes.

Turning to Tommy, Grandma reached down, resting her hands on his.

"Tommy, what a blessing you have given us and your community."

"Don't thank me, ma'am. Thank God. It is His gift."

"Yes, I know that. Your sister told us about the struggles you've had, and yet you've allowed yourself to be used for this—this wonderful portrayal of Jesus's suffering."

Tommy was a man of few words, partly because it was difficult for him to speak. Usually his artwork did the talking.

"I was an angry boy for a long time after my accident. I became bitter and selfish. Nothing mattered but my self-pity. I couldn't understand. I didn't try to understand. My family was patient with me and kind to me. Then one day, I read a verse that set me on the path to turning things around."

"What was it?" Grandma asked.

Slowly and with difficulty, Tommy spoke the words that had awakened his spirit.

> "When His greatness met my weakness,
> When His blood surged through my soul,
> When His Love destroyed my hatred,
> Jesus washed me white as snow."

Tears were trickling down Tommy's face. No one spoke. Then Tommy raised his hand. Trembling, he pointed toward the painting. When everyone had his or her eyes focused on the painting, he spoke again.

"If He could go through all that," Tommy paused a few seconds before continuing, "then I can go through this."

"Let's see, we'll plan on eating breakfast about eight o'clock in the morning," Mr. VanCortland said. "That should give us plenty of time to finish what we need to and still allow us to get to the prison about one o'clock. Isn't that the time you need to be there?"

"Yes, it is," Joe replied. "But let us take you out for breakfast tomorrow. You've done plenty for us already. Surely there's a nice restaurant nearby."

This time Sharon's mother answered.

"Well, yes, there is a nice restaurant uptown, but I already have breakfast casseroles ready. We can visit and enjoy each other's company easier here."

"If I were you, Dad," chimed Jessie, "I'd take her up on it. She's well known for her breakfast casseroles."

"Okay, it's settled then," said Thomas. "How did you like sleeping downstairs in Tommy's old room last night, A. J.?"

"It was great. You know, after getting to know Tommy, I think I'm going to enjoy it even more tonight."

"Good, I'm glad you enjoyed it. I'm happy you enjoyed meeting Tommy too. I'll tell you another thing; he enjoyed being with all of you. He rarely speaks to anyone as much as he did you folks tonight. Thanks for being here."

"This entire weekend has been a real treat, Mr. VanCortland. I am getting a bit tired, though. I think I'll head off to bed."

"Suit yourself, A. J. Get a good night's rest. We'll see you in the morning."

A. J. felt like he was staying in a celebrity's room. It felt good to relax with the memory of Tommy.

All the happenings of the last two days and the apprehension of what might happen on the morrow kept sleep at a distance. His mind catapulted from scene to scene, each one bringing a voice from the past.

> *Someday, I hope you find the perfect law of liberty, A. J.*
> *Father, forgive them, for they know not what they do!*
> *Our fathers, chained in prisons dark, were still in heart*
>   *and conscience free.*
> *My God, my God, why hast thou forsaken me?*
> *Liberty is like a butterfly.*
> *I'm not at all surprised, Aaron. I always knew you*
>   *could do it.*
> *It is finished!*
> *A house divided against itself cannot stand.*
> *If He could go through all that, I can go through this.*

At long last, A. J.'s mind could rest. He drifted off to sleep.

"That night is like a blur in my memory." Jacob Bensley spoke freely, but softly. "It's true; I didn't help myself by drinking. I've regretted those events over and over …"

A. J. stared straight ahead, afraid his thoughts would be obvious if he moved. Since the moment they had entered a small room connecting the lobby with the prison cells, his mind was a mirage of stampeding horses, churning up dust, distorting reality.

The heavy metal door had slammed behind them with a thud of finality. The four visitors stood without speaking in the small elevator-like room. A door on the opposite side opened. They entered a larger room, divided with a steel partition containing thick safety glass. They were invited to sit at a table placed against the window.

Joe sat in a chair on the left end of the table. Grandma sat next to him, then Jessie, and A. J. on the right end. Faint sounds of doors opening and closing echoed somewhere in the building.

A door opened on the opposite side of the room. They watched two guards enter as they escorted a prisoner to the separation wall of thick glass. The guards spoke five words before leaving:

"You've got twenty minutes, Bensely."

The four sat expectantly, watching the inmate whose head was slightly bowed. When he looked up, A. J. saw eyes brimming with kindness. That didn't mesh at all with the boy's preconception.

Jacob had taken the initiative to begin. He thanked each one for coming; then he apologized for all the agony he had caused, even for the inconvenience of them coming to see him. He spoke freely, but softly.

"I know there is nothing I can do to change anything that happened. All I can offer is my apology and ask—"

"Mr. Bensely," Grandma interrupted, "I don't know why, but I have this urge to ask a question. May I?"

"Sure."

"You were a pretty long way from your home that night. Why were you in our community?"

"My life had fallen apart, ma'am."

"How?"

"Well, when I got home from work that evening and our dog wasn't running down the driveway to meet me, I could sense something was wrong. I soon discovered the reason when I entered the house and found the note from my wife."

"What was on the note?" asked Grandma.

"She was leaving me."

"Did she say why?"

"She didn't have to. It had been building for quite a long while. But I don't want to bore you with details of my life."

"Please continue," Jessie entreated. "I'm interested."

Jacob took the nodding heads, even a slight movement from A. J., as encouragement to continue.

"Our family lived in a well-to-do section of town. My wife and I had twin daughters in high school and one six-year-old son. As you can imagine, he was the apple of our eye. The entire family adored him.

"On a warm Saturday afternoon about six years ago, this secure world started to unravel. I was working outside, and little Joey was playing nearby. He loved to play around the bushes that were about ten feet from the road, but he was always very careful about not going on the road."

Anticipating the drama about to unfold, Joe interrupted, "Mr. Bensely, you don't need to continue if it's too painful."

"No, no. It's okay," Jacob reassured him.

"I heard this deep, menacing growl. Before I could react to Joey's frightened scream, a stray dog had leaped on him. Had I not been as close as I was, the dog would have mangled him beyond recognition. As it was, the injuries were limited to four deep skin wounds. The damage was done, however. Infection set in. Despite the antibiotics and medical interventions, our beautiful boy passed from this life within a week."

A somber mood united the two rooms as Jacob struggled to keep his composure.

"I know my time with you is limited, so I'll try to make a long story shorter."

Grandma wiped tears and signaled for him to continue.

"The dog was not rabid. We'll never know what provoked the attack. After the initial grieving period, I became the target of my family's anger. In their eyes, it was my fault, you see, that little Joey was attacked by the dog. It was my fault that little Joey lost his life.

"Over the next year and a half, we communicated less and less. Then I learned my wife was seeing another man. We lived with this precarious arrangement for six more months. I always hoped she would reconsider and accept me again. Then came that awful Friday night when I read the note.

"I was done. I was spent. I didn't care what happened. I was not a drinking man, but that night I became one. I just started driving east, stopping occasionally to visit another tavern.

"Then the rain started coming. The rain, the alcohol, and my attitude did not make a good combination. We all know what happened next."

"I'm so sorry to hear all the troubles you had," Grandma interjected. "Sometimes life just seems to be nearly unbearable."

"The first two years in prison were beyond miserable," Jacob continued. "I felt sorry for myself every day, directing blame and anger toward everyone and everything.

"Then one day, out of sheer boredom, I attended a prison ministry class. What could be the harm? I thought. At least it will get me out of this cell. I wasn't ready for what I received. The people talking to us seemed very convincing and genuine. They appeared to really believe what they were saying. I decided to check it out a little closer.

"The Bible they gave me became a constant companion. The more I read, the more I wanted to read. I memorized verses. Things started to click and make sense. I began to see myself in the light of the scriptures. Previously, I had always thought I was Mr. Right, but I was really Mr. Wrong, as wrong as wrong could be.

"All my life, I had never paid attention to the Bible. If anything, I looked at it as another book of fiction. But with a lot of study and guidance from people who really cared, I discovered the fountain of redemption through the blood of our Savior."

"You seem very contented," Joe observed.

"I am, Mr. Franklin. But, believe me, I wasn't always this way. I was one of the bitterest people here."

"How did your change come about?" The words slipped out of A. J. before he gave much thought.

"Thanks for asking that, son. It's the greatest transformation I've ever experienced. One of the young men in our study group pointed out the verse that says, 'God resisteth the proud, but giveth grace to the humble.' No wonder I was floundering. I was so proud. Now I wanted God's help so badly."

He paused to dry his eyes and clear his thoughts. Grandma could hardly speak, so Jessie asked the obvious. "How did you find God's grace?"

"I prayed—real hard—for a humble mind. I poured out the rottenness of my past life to a trusted believer. He advised me to forgive my wife, even the man she married, and any who had trespassed against me. It was difficult, but God helped me succeed. Then he said you must also forgive yourself. In time, I was able to forgive everyone, even myself. Then, one morning, I can't even explain it, but everything changed. It felt like freedom! Free from every evil thought, free from all that was sour in this life!

"Walking in the prison yard that morning, it was like the Lord told me to look up. I looked up and there was a butterfly floating peacefully in the breeze. Now, I'd seen butterflies before, but none that captivated me like that one. I know God speaks to people in different ways, but for me it was like He was telling me through that butterfly that everything is okay. I fell to my knees, privately weeping with thanksgiving."

Jessie's hand found A. J.'s and squeezed it.

After a few moments, Jacob continued. "Now I just want to make this complete by asking your forgiveness."

At that moment the heavy door swung open.

"Time's up, Bensely."

Jacob started to get up, but a voice stopped him. It was A. J.'s voice, like an arrow of sunlight piercing a dense fog.

"Sirs, I understand you have a schedule and a job to do. But could we have just three more minutes—so we can pray together?"

The guards stared at the five faces streaked with trails of tears. They looked at each other and shrugged.

"Okay. Three minutes. No more!"

The door slammed behind them.

The five looked at one another with compassionate smiles. A. J. spoke quietly.

"Dad, would you entreat the Lord and give Him thanks?"

An Old Acquaintance

The door to Mr. Harnel's classroom was open. A. J. entered and sat in the same seat he had used during his junior year. Like an old friend from the past, the chair massaged his memory.

"Well, what do we have here, a new student for American History I?" Mr. Harnel was chipper as he walked into the room.

"No, but sometimes I wish I was taking it again. It was probably my favorite class. It seems there's so much I need to learn yet."

"Thanks for the compliment. You're going to miss the bus, though, aren't you?"

"That's okay. I drove to school today. I'm going to stay over and work on the speech. That's only two weeks away, you know."

"That's right, isn't it? How's the paper coming?"

"OK, I guess. But I'm starting to get cold feet."

"Cold feet?"

"Well, not really cold feet, I guess. It's just that I don't know if I'm really the one to do this or not. I don't know if all those people will be interested in the things that are important to me."

"Let me tell you one thing, A. J. You just speak from your heart, and the people will appreciate it."

"That could be, I guess. But, really, I've been wondering if you have a Plan B."

"Plan B? What are you talking about?"

"Well, if I decide I don't want to go ahead with it, do you have something else to turn to?"

"If you had asked that a month ago, maybe we would have been able to find another program. But not now. It's too late to switch gears. As the old saying goes, you're the only game in town a week from this Saturday evening."

"I just don't know if I can do the job," A. J. murmured.

"Look at me." Mr. Harnel's voice resonated with a sterling sound.

"I've heard people on the street talking about how they're looking forward to this weekend. And a lot of that is because *you* are speaking. A. J., remember this one thing: speak from your heart!"

Their eyes held each other about five seconds. Then Mr. Harnel changed the subject.

"Look, I've got to attend a department head meeting. It will last about an hour. You can use my room to study if you want to."

"Swell. I appreciate that."

"Just close the door when you leave."

Coach McCulloh was just beginning after-school basketball practice in the gymnasium. The rhythmic sound of bouncing balls from the first floor provided a relaxing atmosphere as A. J. began his study. Deep in thought, he was slightly startled when he noticed someone standing in the doorway, looking intently at him.

"Tyler! What's up?"

"I was just on my way to basketball practice when I saw you sitting here. I didn't mean to frighten you."

"You didn't, actually. I was just surprised to see it was you standing there."

"Why?"

"I figured you had written me off a long time ago."

"What makes you think that?"

"Oh, it just seems like everything you do turns out so well—football and basketball star, popular, good grades."

"You said it about right, man. It just seems that way."

"Oh, come on, Tyler. You know it's true. And your folks have always had plenty of money. What more do you need?"

"I guess you're right in one sense. I have been rather fortunate. But there is one more thing I need, and only you can give it to me."

A. J. sat back in his chair, looking with amazement at his classmate.

"Well, now, this does beat all. Tyler Renken, the man of many talents, needing something from me, A. J. Franklin?"

"I'm serious, A. J. I'm glad for the chance happening of meeting you here today alone so we can talk."

"You are serious, aren't you?"

"I've never been more serious in my life."

"Well, what could you possibly need that I can give you?"

Tyler glanced at the open door and then stepped over to close it.

"Can I sit down?"

"Sure, help yourself."

Making himself comfortable, Tyler stared at the floor a few long seconds before making eye contact.

"Your forgiveness."

"My ... forgiveness?"

"You'll never know, A. J., the agony I've gone through these past four years since the night ... well, I'm sure you remember."

"Sure, sure," A. J. responded in an unbelieving tone.

"I was so egotistical," Tyler continued, "so self-centered. I couldn't believe someone could be better than me. Then when word came back of your accident, and worse yet that your mother didn't survive, it was like somebody stabbed me. It's time to pull the knife out."

There was a long pause as the two boys looked at each other.

"I had no idea, Tyler. It just always seemed you were in control of your life."

"I know it looked that way. But inside I've been pretty torn up. Oh, there are times I can play the macho part. Times I can almost convince myself I'm really somebody. But more and more I see myself as nothing more than a crummy poacher, always stepping on someone to make myself look better. I want to change all that. I need to start with you."

"I've got nothing to offer, Tyler."

"Oh, yes you do. You've got more than you realize. I've been watching you, A. J., ever since the accident. You've made such a comeback. Sometimes I envy you. The committee made a wise selection when they chose you to give the Veterans Day talk. You're the best we've got."

A. J. got up and walked to the window. He gazed out over the campus. He watched a few of the remaining worn-out leaves occasionally drift to the ground and knew the replacement bud was already there ready to bloom when spring arrived. Softly, almost as though he was talking to the window, he spoke.

"Do you remember, Tyler, raking leaves together into huge piles?"

"For sure, man. Then wrestling in the crunching leaves until they were scattered again."

"Or how about the year we had the big snow, and the forts we built," A. J. mused.

Tyler laughed.

"Don't forget our snowball stash we used on unsuspecting victims."

A. J. continued looking out the window, slowly shaking his head. When he turned around, Tyler had gotten up from his chair. Warm remembrances had softened his countenance.

"Four years," A. J. whispered.

Tyler's brow furrowed before A. J. spoke again.

"Four years we've wasted."

"I know," Tyler rejoined. "It was my fault. I'm sorry."

"Don't shoulder all the blame, Tyler. It was just a careless, youthful comment. I let it eat on me too much and tried to avoid you."

"Can we recapture the goodness of life, A. J.?"

A. J.'s far away gaze nearly startled his friend.

115

"Do you know what I'm thinking right now, Tyler?"

"I couldn't guess!"

"I'm thinking back to the sixth grade. The teacher made us read a book about a certain fish somewhere on the West Coast. We weren't too thrilled but she got so enthused telling us about it. What was the name of that fish?"

"I think it was Pacific something, wasn't it?"

"Oh, yeah, that's it—Pacific salmon! It's coming back to me now. The eggs would hatch in freshwater mountain streams. Then the young fish would slowly float downstream, eating and growing. In time, they made it to the salty ocean waters. They would swim and live for years in the ocean."

"I remember it now, A. J. At the right time, they came back to the freshwater mountain stream to lay their eggs, many to the same stream where they were born."

"As I think about it now, Tyler, that is simply amazing. And if that fish can find its way back, I see no reason why we can't go back to the friendship of our youth!"

The two met with a solid handshake and overdue embrace. Tyler looked appreciatively at his newly regained pal.

"Well, I'd better hurry on to practice. The tournament begins Friday night."

"Give 'em a good one, Ty."

"I'll try. You sharpen your speech for next weekend. Show them what our generation is all about—that we're ready to pick up where they left off."

Tyler turned to leave.

"By the way, Tyler, I'm getting some classmates to help that evening. Would you be interested?"

"If there's any way I could help, A. J., I'd love to. That is, if I can do a suitable job. I wouldn't want to ruin anything."

"I'm not worried about you messing up. How 'bout if we get together tomorrow over lunch and I'll explain it to you?"

"Count me in, A. J. I'll be there."

TRACES OF LIBERTY

"You're not eating much, A. J.," Grandma observed.

"I'll eat more later this evening," A. J. said, laughing, "when I can enjoy it."

"We're anxious to hear your talk, A. J.," Mr. VanCortland said. "Your sister has given you quite an advance billing."

"I hope she didn't overdo it. Thanks for coming. I wish Tommy could have come with you."

"Thanks for thinking of him, A. J.," Sharon's mother added. "He wishes he could be here. It's so difficult for someone in his situation to travel this far. We'll take a program announcement to him and tell him all about it."

"I understand this is quite a tradition in your town," Mr. VanCortland observed. "Are you responsible for all this good food, Grandma?"

"Oh, no, not hardly. Everyone does his or her share in bringing it. In answer to your first comment, I think this is our twentieth year. We started it two years after the big war. People of Bridges figured this was one way to show our appreciation for those who served in defense of freedom. The date was changed a few years back and a speech from a high school senior was added; otherwise, it's about like it was when we started."

"Bridges! That's a unique name for a town." Anthony VanCortland smiled while looking around the table. "I don't recall seeing bodies of water near here when we came today." He turned to Doc Roberts, who was sitting next to him. "What's the history behind that name?"

"I'm going to volley that question to our historian across the table. Judge knows more about this town than anyone."

"You flatter me, Doc. But I do get enthused when I talk about Bridges. You're right, Anthony. There are no notable bodies of water here. And there are no historic structural bridges here, either."

"Let me guess, then," the college president interrupted. "Bridges must be a symbolic name."

"Keep going; you're on the right track."

"That's where my vision ends," Anthony replied. "I'll wait quietly now for your expertise."

"The symbolism dates back to the Civil War era. Our state, you see, was once a part of Virginia."

The president raised his eyebrows. "I didn't know that!"

"Yes, and just as a sidelight, did you know that when the Civil War began, President Lincoln asked one of Virginia's favorite sons to lead his army?"

"Really? Who was that?"

"I'm going to let A. J. tell you. He did a research paper on the man."

A. J. was surprised, but he didn't mind joining the conversation.

"This man was the son of a Revolutionary War hero. He graduated second in his class at West Point and was rapidly becoming one of the best military men in America—General Robert E. Lee."

"Oh, of course. I should have known that! Obviously, he turned President Lincoln down."

"You're correct. When Virginia voted to secede from the Union, the honorable general said that even though he didn't support slavery or secession, he couldn't turn his back on his state and family."

"That must have been quite a blow for the president."

"It was. He said he lost a man worth fifty thousand soldiers."

Everyone at the table seemed to enjoy the history lesson. Buoyed by their rapt attention, Judge Evans took up the reins again.

"It must have been horrible for the state at that time, because a lot of people in the western part of Virginia did not support secession. Emotions ran so deep that it wasn't long before these people wanted statehood. In 1863, during the middle of the war, this section of the state broke away, and West Virginia was admitted to the Union."

"Interesting," the president mused. "But how does the name Bridges figure in?"

"Well, the town was founded twelve years later in 1875, near the border of the two states. Considering all that the nation had just gone through, the town fathers thought Bridges was a fitting name, kind of a connecting link for two eras."

"If I may," Doc Roberts volunteered, "I'd like to add an important fact to this conversation. Our people take this history very seriously. This evening is an outgrowth of that bridging spirit we enjoy yet today."

Judge Evans took special note of Anthony's deep concentration.

"Amazing," Anthony replied softly. "And very fitting."

Then, as an afterthought, he continued slowly. "Isn't it peculiar that your state joined the Union during a crisis in 1863? Exactly one hundred years later, another crisis shook our nation when President John F. Kennedy was assassinated." He thought a moment. "I remember what I was doing then, as do most people who were old enough to realize what had happened."

"It's strange you should bring that up," Grandma interjected, "because four years ago, our Veterans Day celebration was canceled on that unforgettable weekend."

A sudden silence draped the table.

"That wasn't the reason, however, that this event was cancelled," Grandma continued. "The real reason was that our lovely Loretta was taken from this life that same day."

Mrs. VanCortland quickly interrupted.

"I'm sorry. That wasn't very considerate of us."

119

"That's okay," A. J. responded. "It is a tough memory, that's for sure. But, in a way, it helps to put us in the proper mood, to remind us how serious this evening is. My talk will venture a little into that area."

"Well," Doc Roberts interrupted, "I hope the mood is set. The mayor is walking to the podium."

"It is my privilege to welcome each of you here this evening. When I was asked to take this position, I agreed to do it for three or four years. This is my fifteenth year, and I'm still not ready to give it up. Every celebration seems to have a special flavor to it.

"Before we recognize our veterans, Richard Brewster has asked to share something that has been on his heart. Richard, take as much time as you need."

Mr. Brewster cautiously approached the podium. Then he turned to address the gathering. He used no notes.

"I am pleased to see a good representation of both young and older people here tonight. Some of you may not know me. I fought in Europe during World War II. Our country was united and we accomplished the goal of helping to end the war. When we came back to the states, it was like coming home to a hero's welcome. Everyone was so appreciative.

"Many thought it would be the war to end all wars. Unfortunately, we were mistaken. Oppressive governments continue to terrorize and oppress people wherever they can. For the past two years, we have been gradually building a larger military presence in the little country of Vietnam. Many of us never even knew of this place ten years ago. Today, it is a household name.

"It's a different type of war. Things are not going as well as we expected. Some are questioning if we even have the will to win. With increasing taxes needed to support the conflict, a general unrest begins to rumble throughout America.

"You may know someone who has served there or is going. I know some from our community are there now. Perhaps some from our senior class are contemplating entering one of the service branches. That is commendable.

"As a seasoned veteran, I make a couple requests from everyone here. Please keep them in your prayers, and as they return, when they do, grant them the same respect you showed to us when we returned from World War II. They deserve nothing less. Thank you."

A somber moment of reflection followed. Then the applause began, quietly at first, building to a crescendo of appreciative warmth.

"Thank you, Richard, for your words of consideration. In uncertain times like these, we need to stick together. Your words provide a fitting background for recognition of our veterans here tonight.

"Would those of you that have served our country please stand? Turn and face the different sections of the audience so that you may see them, and they may see you."

A hearty applause echoed in the auditorium. When they were seated, the applause continued while the remainder of the people arose out of respect for the heralded group of veterans.

"Thank you very much. Now, would the widows and children of deceased veterans please stand?"

A smaller group stood. But the applause was even stronger than before.

"Again, thank you. Our prayers and continued warm wishes remain with each one."

A. J. glanced nervously around his table as the time drew closer for him to take the microphone. To him, the table was filled with celebrities. His father, Joe, and Grandma were surrounded on either side by Doc and his wife and Judge Evans with his wife. Following around the circular table sat Jessie and Sharon and Sharon's parents.

"A. J. Franklin has agreed to be our senior class presenter tonight. Before he speaks, we have a special added touch. His sister, Jessie, and her college roommate, Sharon VanCortland, will be singing a special selection."

THE PERFECT LAW

T he brunette/blonde duet positioned themselves behind the podium. Their mellow voices delivered a stirring rendition of "America the Beautiful." Amateur photographers hurried to capture the essence of the moment before deafening applause escorted the girls back to their chairs.

The gymnasium took on an unusual quietness as A. J. Franklin, the boy whose life had been an open book to the community, made his way to the front. Setting his notes on the podium, he looked out at the crowd.

"The words of the second verse we just heard sung remind us why we are here tonight:

> O beautiful for pilgrim feet,
> Whose stern impassion'd stress,
> A thoroughfare for freedom beat,
> Across the wilderness.

"Coupled with the continued efforts to preserve freedom, it helps us realize how fortunate we are.

"Four years ago this weekend, President John Kennedy was assassinated. A paragraph from his inaugural speech lends credence to America's founding ideals.

> Let every nation know, whether it wishes us well or
> ill, that we shall pay any price, bear any burden, meet
> any hardship, support any friend, oppose any foe to
> insure the survival and the success of liberty.

"Four years ago, the same day JFK was assassinated, my mother died in an automobile accident. She was the first to make me aware of the phrase, 'the perfect law of liberty.' It is easy to locate those words in James, a book of the Bible. Incorporating the principles of this perfect law into our lives, however, is a much more difficult task.

"The youngsters standing off to my left are fourth graders from our local school. They helped design the front of programs you will receive. We'll give them a couple minutes to pass these to you."

While the fourth graders delivered programs to the audience, seven classmates came to the front tables and sat with A. J. Whispers of anticipation rifled through the gymnasium. Soon everyone quieted as A. J. again stepped behind the podium.

"The seven people who have joined me are my classmates. Each of them will talk about one of the topics on the program. If you haven't already, turn to the inside of the program brochure, and you will see their names listed beside their respective topic."

1. Proclaiming Liberty ....Jeff Coates
2. Birth of America...................................Georgia Landrum
3. A House Divided ....Brenda Schuster
4. Humility..Ron Billington
5. A New Beginning................................Lauren Masterson
6. Sacrifice ....Patricia Carlson
7. Forgiveness & Charity ....Tyler Renken

"At first glance, this may appear to be a curious mixture of topics. It's strange, but these topics seemed to flow automatically without our prompting. I'm reminded of words spoken by Abraham Lincoln during the heart of the Civil War: 'I claim not to have controlled events, but confess plainly that events have controlled me.'

"We never outlined our presentation like this in the beginning. Liberty, of course, was to be our theme. Then it just seemed to take on a life of its own, leading us from one step to the next.

"The very first topic led us to the Bible. From that point on, we could not escape taking note of similarities.

"We were amazed that many of the principles of America's founding and continued growth seemed to parallel certain principles of the Bible. None of the Americans named are meant to be likened to any personalities of the Bible. They just happened to be the ones who appeared during that time in history.

"Jeff is our first speaker."

(Jeff's Response)

"Our defining moment happened almost immediately. While looking together at a picture of the Liberty Bell, Lauren raised a question about words inscribed on the bell. None of us had an answer, so we researched the topic.

"We were surprised to find the verse on the bell had been borrowed from the Old Testament, Leviticus 25:10: 'Proclaim liberty throughout the land unto all the inhabitants thereof.' We further found this bell had been cast in the 1750s and was rung every year from 1776 until 1835 to commemorate the Declaration of Independence. A crack in the bell prevented its ringing thereafter.

"If colonial leaders and our Founding Fathers revered a verse of scripture to elevate it to such heights, we reasoned, what else might the Bible say about liberty? Our thirst wasn't quenched until we searched, finding gems such as: 'and where the Spirit of the Lord is, there is liberty' (2 Corinthians 3:17), 'to proclaim liberty to the captives' (Isaiah 61:1), 'the glorious liberty of the children of God'

(Romans 8:21), 'Stand fast, therefore, in the liberty wherewith Christ hath made us free' (Galatians 5:1), and 'I will walk at liberty: for I seek thy precepts' (Psalm 119:45)."

Jeff paused a few moments to allow the audience to think about what he had said.

"We were hooked. There was no turning back from our quest for liberty. It appeared to us that the Bible's author wanted mankind to embrace liberty.

"It's no secret to those who have studied history that liberty has been a scarce commodity worldwide. Then, to the surprise of many established countries, a group of patriots along the eastern coast of America seemed determined to blaze a new trail. Thomas Jefferson penned momentous words in the Declaration of Independence:

> We hold these truths to be self evident, that all men are created equal, that they are endowed by their Creator with certain unalienable Rights, that among these are Life, Liberty, and the pursuit of Happiness.

"Nearly two hundred years have gone by since the beginning of that experiment involving thirteen independent colonies. Our nation has prospered to become the world leader. It seemed more than coincidental to us.

"Understanding that liberty was to be foundational in this new government, and noting that liberty was a theme in the Bible, we wondered how influential the Bible was in developing the United States. Our research was explosive. At times, we felt like archaeologists unearthing treasures buried by winds of time and neglect."

"Thanks, Jeff. As we discovered, our Founding Fathers had all the bases covered, so to speak. They were educated in Greek, Roman, and European history; they were versed in the classics and well acquainted with the Bible. From all these sources, they pulled together the best precepts to develop this government that has served as a beacon of liberty," A. J. concluded.

"That leads to our next topic. Georgia, you're up."

(Georgia's Response)

"I'm happy for this opportunity. My special interest is America's beginning, possibly because Georgia was the name of one of the colonies. My main interest, however, developed because of inconsistencies I noticed while studying about it in grade school. The most glaring inequity I found was between the ideal expressed in the Declaration of Independence and the way things really were in the colonies."

Wrinkled brows appeared in the audience. The Declaration of Independence had always been spoken of reverently, not the way this young lady was talking.

"As Jeff already highlighted in quoting Jefferson, the Declaration stated that all men are created equal and endowed by their creator with the unalienable rights of life, liberty, and the pursuit of happiness. And yet, at the same time, this group of thirteen colonies sported an amazing number of people held as slaves. Being an idealistic youngster, my mind wanted to know how this could be.

"I soon regretted being so judgmental. Our founders had not ignored this issue. Slavery was a problem they did not create; it was inherited, an institution that had taken root more than one hundred fifty years earlier at Jamestown. They realized that trying to suddenly uproot slavery would eliminate any chance to unify the colonies. In its infancy, the republic could not effectively deal with it.

"We began to see certain similarities to our own lives. The United States of America was born with a blueprint for liberty. The blueprint, however, was smudged with slavery, to the tune of nearly five hundred thousand slaves.

"We are born into this world with a blueprint for liberty endowed by our creator. This blueprint is also smudged by a stain—the stain of unrighteousness acquired years earlier from the fall in the Garden of Eden.

"Both entities are born with great potential, but also an inherited disadvantage. Neither is able to deal effectively with that disadvantage during infancy. The discrepancy grows toward a future confrontation.

"I would like to conclude my remarks with a quote from George Washington: 'I can only say that there is not a man living who wishes more sincerely than I do to see a plan adopted for the abolition of it [slavery].'"

"'That's an interesting observation, Georgia," stated A. J. "Our next speaker, Brenda, will move us through the founding of our nation to a watershed moment in America, the Civil War."

(Brenda's Response)

"Unable to rid the country of slavery, our Founding Fathers did, however, attempt to inhibit the growth of it. In 1787, the Continental Congress established the Northwest Territory. Slavery was to be prohibited in this territory, which eventually became the states of Ohio, Indiana, Illinois, Michigan, Wisconsin, and part of Minnesota. They had also set 1800 as the date to outlaw foreign slave trade. Two states pressured Congress to delay that law eight years. So, in 1808, Congress passed the law to outlaw the foreign slave trade. Interestingly, the following year of 1809 welcomed the birth of a lad in Kentucky, Abraham Lincoln.

"From its founding until 1861, America played both sides of the slavery issue, trying to satisfy all interests. Compromises and bargaining kept an uneasy peace in the nation. The Missouri Compromise of 1820 effectively kept slavery within its current boundaries.

"In 1856, Stephen A. Douglas maneuvered the Kansas-Nebraska Act through Congress. This nullified the Missouri Compromise and threatened to spread slavery westward.

"Lincoln, who had been in and out of politics since 1832, reentered the political arena with a passion. His famous 'House Divided' speech propelled him to national prominence: 'A house divided against itself cannot stand. I do not expect the Union to fall. Either it will become all one or all the other.' The nation listened. In 1860, he was elected president.

"Many years earlier, Jesus had spoken similar words to his contemporaries: 'A house divided against itself cannot stand.' In another place, he said, 'No man can serve two masters: for either he will hate the one, and love the other; or else he will hold to the one, and despise the other. Ye cannot serve God and mammon,'" she concluded.

"Very interesting, Brenda. Thank you." A. J. turned to the audience. "I want to again make it clear that we are not attempting to compare Abraham Lincoln or anyone else with Jesus of the Bible. They had different missions on earth. What we want to emphasize, however, are the Scriptural attributes many of our leaders used while guiding the country.

"We're just about at the halfway point. Ron will talk to us about the fourth concept, humility."

(Ron's Response)

Ron took his place behind the podium. As he prepared to speak, a sharp voice from the audience shattered the stillness.

"If I would have known we were going to have church all evening, I might not have come! I think you're getting plenty heavy with the Bible. In light of the recent court rulings, carrying on like this looks kind of risky."

Murmuring voices could be heard. A. J. started to get up from his chair. Before he could, another man rose to speak. His calm, deep voice with a slow drawl permeated the room.

"I've been farming in this community well over thirty years. I served in World War II. I remember JFK's assassination like it was yesterday. America's been good for me and my family, and from what I read and hear, she's done a lot for people around the world too.

"Yes, I know that a few years ago a ruling came down that we can no longer have prayers in school. For the life of me, I cannot figure out why. It seems to me our country has done well with a little religion in our schools for over one hundred seventy-five years. Why is it wrong now? I hope we're not putting our country in jeopardy by doing this. It kind of worries me.

"Be that as it may, these young folks are not asking anyone to pray. Everything they are saying ties in with our history. Think of the places they could be or what they could be doing tonight. Instead, they are here talking about things that really mean something. So they're talking about things in the Bible. What harm is that?

"This is one of the most refreshing evenings I've had in a long time. I say let them continue. We might all learn something."

Led by college President VanCortland, a healthy applause swept through the audience. Tensions dissolved. A. J. remained seated. His classmate continued the program.

"Liberty—we cannot quench our thirst for it. Our pursuit will not end with this evening, but we have found enough to set us on the right path. When we came across this next piece of information, we all felt it had a place in this presentation.

"It is a poem that became one of Lincoln's favorites. I'm only going to read one stanza because it is part of a longer poem called 'Mortality.'

> Oh! why should the spirit of mortal be proud?
> Like a swift-fleeting meteor, a fast flying cloud
> A flash of the lightning, a break of the wave
> He passeth from life to his rest in the grave.
> Oh! why should the spirit of mortal be proud?

"A verse in the New Testament states, 'God giveth grace to the humble, but he resisteth the proud.' Many instances lead us to believe Lincoln was a humble person. He was well acquainted with the Bible and its precepts. Having no false illusions about himself or his position, he recognized he was only an instrument and that God was in control. At one point, when the war was going badly for the North, the president was asked whether he thought the Lord was on his side. Lincoln responded, 'That's not what concerns me. What does concern me is if I am on His side.'

"The war with its casualties weighed heavily on this man. He acknowledged he had gone to his knees many times, recognizing that was the only place to turn."

"Thanks, Ron. When thinking about humility, I'm reminded of this, which Lincoln said: 'As I would not be a slave, so I would not be a master.' To me that sounds a lot like the Golden Rule from the New Testament, 'Do unto others as you would have them do unto you.'

"Our next speaker, Lauren, talks about a new beginning."

(Lauren's Response)

"Every morning on my way to school, I drive past a beautiful meadow. For whatever reason, one corner of that meadow had been severely neglected last year. By fall, it was a combination of tangled weeds and unwanted plants. This spring, that section of dry, tangled weeds and plants was burned away. I had never before seen that done. I wondered why the farmer wanted to destroy a section of his field in that manner. Within a month, I received an answer. That scorched plot of earth transformed to a brilliant emerald green as the plants returned with new life.

"After sharing this new beginning for that plot of land, others in our group were reminded of similar happenings. One mentioned a phrase used by Abraham Lincoln in his Gettysburg Address. He ended that memorable speech with the confident declaration: 'that we here highly resolve that these dead shall not have died in vain; that this nation shall have a new birth of freedom; and that this government of the people, by the people, for the people, shall not perish from the earth.'

"America already possessed freedom, but this would be a new birth of freedom. It was made possible only after our nation had been dragged through a bitter war resulting in the deaths of six hundred thousand people.

"Then another classmate recalled the story of a man named Nicodemus coming to Jesus by night with questions:

"Many years ago, shortly before the Crucifixion, a man named Nicodemus came to Jesus by night with questions that troubled him. Jesus responded, 'Except a man be born again, he cannot see the kingdom of God.' Of course, Nicodemus had already been born once. The opportunity to be born again had not existed until Jesus had taken upon himself the sin and unrighteousness of the world, suffered severely at the hands of men, and been crucified."

Lauren allowed a few seconds of silence before finishing.

"Removing obstacles of the past through a severe cleansing allows for a new beginning, a new birth."

"Lauren has shared a pivotal concept with us," A. J. said. "Tremendous sacrifice is required to gain anything this precious. Patricia will speak about that."

(Patricia's Response)

"Nothing worthwhile was ever gained without some type of sacrifice. I was moved by Mr. Brewster's words earlier this evening. He and others here tonight could teach us about sacrifice. They know what it means to lose one's identity, while decisions from the top dictate their actions. Am I right, Richard?"

The seasoned veteran soberly nodded his agreement.

Patricia continued, "Whether it was storming the beaches at Normandy or trudging across an open field with Pickett's Charge at Gettysburg, there was no option. The astronomical odds of certain death did not exempt the soldier from participation. His will was not his own.

"The prophet Isaiah was given a vision years before it happened concerning Jesus's sacrifice to complete God's plan of redemption: 'He was wounded for our transgressions, he was bruised for our iniquity, the chastisement of our peace was laid upon him, and by his stripes we are healed.' Jesus sacrificed His all.

"A tremendous sacrifice was also made in the struggle to gain the soul of America. Huge stores of wealth were destroyed in that conflict. As you've already been reminded, more than six hundred thousand Americans lost their lives. In the end, even the blood of Lincoln was required.

"Delivering his Second Inaugural Address, President Lincoln put the conflict in perspective: 'Fondly do we hope—fervently do we pray—that this mighty scourge of war may speedily pass away. Yet, if God wills that it continue, until all the wealth piled by the bondman's two hundred and fifty years of unrequited toil shall be sunk, and until every drop of blood drawn with the lash, shall be paid by another drawn with the sword, as was said three thousand years ago, so still it must be said, 'the judgments of the Lord are true and righteous altogether.'"

"We appreciate those insights, Patricia. Lincoln's knowledge of the Bible permeated many of his speeches. The Second Inaugural Address sounded as much like a sermon as it did a political statement. Less than two months later, the entire speech was read at his funeral.

"Tyler also finds the Second Inaugural helpful while weaving forgiveness and charity into our matrix."

(Tyler's Response)

"Many of Lincoln's contemporaries felt that a Northern victory should signal harsh consequences for the states that had seceded. That thinking was not in line with the president's personality nor with his governing style.

"Lincoln was ready for the war to end. He was ready to welcome the Southerners to be countrymen again. He didn't want revenge. A contemporary newsman, Noah Brooks, wrote about Abraham Lincoln: 'He was more devoid of anger, clamor, evil-speaking, and uncharity than any human being I ever knew or heard of.'

"The concluding paragraph of Lincoln's Second Inaugural projected his thoughts toward the close of the war:

> With malice toward none; with charity for all; with firmness in the right, as God gives us to see the right, let us strive on to finish the work we are in; to bind up the nation's wounds; to care for him who shall have borne the battle, and for his widow, and his orphan—to do all which may achieve and cherish a just and lasting peace, among ourselves, and with all nations.

"Had Lincoln lived, forgiveness would have played a big part in the healing of America. Because he was assassinated, however, forgiveness went out the window and America endured too many ugly Reconstruction years.

"The fallen president's wishes were nearly a reflection of the charity that blanketed the land around Jerusalem more than eighteen centuries earlier. Through darkness and storm, a cry that echoes yet today could be heard from the battered and bloodied form on the middle cross: 'Father, forgive them; for they know not what they do.'"

Tyler sat down among his classmates. The band members quietly assumed their positions. A. J. walked to the podium.

"Eight years ago, the poet Carl Sandburg was invited to speak to Congress on the occasion of Abraham Lincoln's one hundred fiftieth birthday anniversary. Speaking of Lincoln, Sandburg said, 'Not often does a man appear on earth who is both velvet and steel.' In retrospect, the same could have been said of Jesus. He preached and practiced love. He wrapped up the entire law with the gentle persuasions of love. Yet, at the same time, He did not yield one inch to unrighteousness. He did not bend or compromise His principles of truth. He willingly endured suffering at the hands of those who hated Him, giving His own life to redeem us, that we would have the opportunity to throw off the shackles of sin and be clothed with His righteousness.

"We, as a group, know that the similarities between political liberty and spiritual liberty go only so far; one is on a much higher plane. The similarities between Abraham Lincoln and Jesus Christ go only so far; Jesus's mission is on a much higher plane.

"The blood that stained our continent was costly and helped preserve America. The blood that stained the Cross unleashed the strength to break the power of evil."

A. J. nodded to his sister. She and Sharon walked to the front of the audience. Without accompaniment, they sang their song for the first time in public:

> Softer than velvet, stronger than steel,
> Now they could see it on Calvary's stark hill;
> Cries of forgiveness blanket the land,
> Tearing the curtain between God and man;
> Thunder and earthquake, blood stains the tree,
> Now, "It is finished," the captives set free;
> Christ reigns triumphant, completing God's Will,
> Softer than velvet, stronger than steel;
> Softer than velvet and stronger than steel.

"Our project has illuminated an erosion of many values that were once highly prized. We seem to be drifting. In his inaugural address,

President Kennedy emphatically declared that we will defeat any foe to defend liberty. We look around and see that no foreign power has conquered us. Could it be that our own self-will is that foe?"

The band began softly playing "The Battle Hymn of the Republic."

"It's time to return to those time-tested values that were anchored in truth. You veterans who we honor this evening have sacrificed too much and have fought too hard to allow those values to fall by the wayside."

The winds' section of the band played softly in the background. Jessie and Sharon began singing the fourth verse:

> In the beauty of the lilies, Christ was born across the sea,
> With a glory in his bosom that transfigured you and me;
> As he died to make men holy, let us live to make men free
> While God is marching on!

The brass instruments joined on the chorus.

> Glory, Glory Hallelujah
> Glory, Glory Hallelujah
> Glory, Glory Hallelujah
> His truth is marching on.

The instrumental band prepared for another round of the chorus. People started standing, joining the two girls in song:

> Glory, Glory Hallelujah
> Glory, Glory Hallelujah

A. J. and his classmates formed a semicircle facing the audience. With misty eyes and heads uplifted, they raised their voices to join with the people of Bridges:

> Glory, Glory Hallelujah, His truth is marching on!

THE RIVER KEEPS FLOWING

S eventh-hour study period was usually a time to finish extra work before the final bell rang. Today, A. J. pushed his homework aside and basked in the memories of the past weekend. What a charge of electricity had gone through the eight seniors! The captivated community continued to buzz over the evening—most of them positively, a few distraught.

A. J. smiled while reminiscing. His reverie was broken when the study hall teacher, Mrs. Wilkey, tapped his shoulder and whispered, "Mr. Cavanaugh would like to see you in his office."

A. J. gathered his books. Walking down the steps, he met Tyler coming to get gym shoes from his locker.

"Hey, A. J.! Leaving early?"

"I wish!"

"Where are you headed with that sour expression?"

"I'm being summoned to the principal's office. No idea what he wants!"

"Uh-oh! I hope it's not what I'm thinking."

"Lay it on me, pal. I'm clueless."

"Just a few minutes ago, I saw three cars pulling into the parking lot. Two men and one woman came up the walk. I remember seeing them some evenings coming to school board meetings after we had finished basketball practice."

"You don't reckon they're coming about this past weekend, do you, Tyler?"

"I don't know why they would. But it looks a little suspicious to me."

"Oh, brother! I'm not looking forward to this."

"Wish I could come with you, pal."

"So do I," A. J. responded dejectedly.

"Hey, A. J.! I was a part of it just like you were. Why couldn't I come with you?"

"I don't know. Let's try it—that is, if you're willing."

"You bet I'm willing. Coach won't mind if I'm late to practice."

Together they continued down the flight of stairs. The door to the office was slightly ajar. A. J. knocked politely. The two youngsters gingerly stepped into the principal's domain.

"Tyler, I'm surprised to see you," Mr. Cavanaugh said with no hesitation. "I didn't know Mrs. Wilkey asked you to come."

"Oh, she didn't, sir. I just met A. J. in the hall, and he told me you wanted to see him. We wondered if it would be okay for me to come with him. If not, I'll leave."

"Oh, no, no! That's quite all right. In fact, it might help our discussion if you are here. Just grab another chair from the outer office. We'll make room for you here."

"Thank you, Mr. Cavanaugh."

Mr. Harnel suggested moving into the conference room where everyone could be comfortably seated around a rectangular table. The three board members, President Jurgens, Miss French, and Mr. Kirgan sat on one side of the table. Across from them sat A. J. and Tyler. The principal and Mr. Harnel sat on opposite ends.

"Well, let's get right to the point. Boys, these board members feel a need to talk about the program Saturday evening."

President Jurgens cleared his throat to speak.

"I must say, boys, we were duly impressed by your knowledge and the presentation. I think your passion touched everyone."

"Thank you, sir," A. J. responded. "I had been counseled to speak from my heart."

Mr. Harnel's slight smile did not escape A. J.'s attention.

"Well," the president continued, "it was obvious each of you spoke with conviction. I appreciated it. Unfortunately, not everyone did."

A. J.'s uncomfortable repositioning caused Tyler to give him a reassuring touch. Slowly, Tyler spoke.

"Could you tell us, sir, what they didn't appreciate?"

"There were just some things that rubbed them the wrong way."

"I kind of gathered that. I was hoping you would be a bit more specific."

"Some people had objections to, well, uh …"

Miss French hurried to help the president.

"I think it was rather obvious that some people objected to references to the Bible."

"Why would they object to that?" A. J. asked with a pained expression. "I thought we had made it rather clear we were trying to paint an actual account of history."

"Since the court ruling a few years ago, officials are watching closely what goes on in our schools."

"This was just a community gathering," A. J. protested. "It wasn't even during school hours!"

The response from the board member was rapid. "It was held on school property!"

"So?"

The pained expression now twisted the president's face.

"Look, boys," he softly said, searching for words, "we just can't afford to run the risk of being, uh, singled out as a district protesting the court ruling."

An uncomfortable silence intervened.

"May I ask another question?"

"Sure, Tyler, go ahead."

"It looked to me like most of the people were singing at the conclusion. It appeared as though they were enjoying it. How many people actually objected to the program?"

"That's not the point," Mr. Kirgan interjected.

"Was it five, ten, twenty, one hundred, or—"

"It doesn't matter," Miss French retorted, "how many there were. We can't go against the law!"

Stopping abruptly, Miss French lowered her voice in apology. "Oh, I'm sorry; I didn't mean to be rude." Looking down at her clasped hands, she continued. "Your program the other evening was very enjoyable. I know most of the people appreciated it. I'm just so sorry it falls on us to enforce this … this ruling, which we have no control over."

A. J. noticed tears welling in her eyes. A somber mood gripped everyone in the room. He found courage to cautiously continue.

"The words of the gentleman who spoke on our behalf keep coming back to me. It was obvious he was disappointed in the court ruling, but he was also concerned about the future. It makes me wonder, too, what will happen in ten to twenty years."

"What are your concerns?" the board president asked.

"There were some things I was going to share with the audience the other night. I didn't because of the one gentleman's objection."

"If you want, you may share them now."

"We probably wouldn't have been so alarmed if we hadn't discovered what we did. It's frightening how far we have drifted. The Founders had a very positive view of education, saying it shall be forever encouraged. They also had a definite philosophy of education. From several sources, stated very clearly in the Northwest Ordinance in particular, we found they always included these three components: religion, morality, and knowledge. There was no mistaking their message."

Following the ensuing silence, Tyler continued the discussion.

"The amazing thing is that these three were always spoken of in that order: religion, morality, and knowledge. We had no doubts that they believed religion produces morality, and morality teaches us how to use knowledge. I, for one, agree with them. Look at how our nation has prospered with that philosophy leading the way. So now I wonder what will happen after we kick the first step out of the ladder."

It was quiet—ever so quiet—maybe thirty seconds, but it seemed a lot longer. Then President Jurgens concluded the meeting, speaking slowly, choosing his words carefully. "I really don't know how to answer you, son. Times are changing. We don't know how far this will go, so we're taking the careful approach. We're going to ask you and your friends to refrain from any organized discussion about these topics at school. What you do outside of school is your business, but don't bring it to school."

"Thanks for walking to the parking lot with me, Tyler. I know Coach is probably expecting you in practice."

"I think he'll understand why I'm late. This is more important right now."

"Well, Ty, he's right about one thing. Times are changing. I probably wouldn't have thought much about it if we hadn't done all that research and discovered things that seem to have been forgotten."

"I know what you mean, A. J. Now that we know, it seems like we should be doing something about it."

"That's what I'm thinking too. But how can we when everything is stacked against us?"

"That song your sister and her friend sang, A. J.—I think we can find a lot of strength in that."

"How so?"

"Well, our approach is definitely going to have to be softer than velvet, but our resolve will need to be stronger than steel."

"Tyler, your reasoning is really taking me off guard, man!"

"It's becoming clearer to me every day now. I'm a little fearful about what could happen."

"For sure. You know, it reminds me of something Thomas Jefferson once said that I think fits this situation also: 'I tremble when I remember our God is a just God.'"

"I think you've nailed it, A. J. Unfortunately, I guess there's not much we can do right now. I'd better get to practice. You ought to come with me. I bet you could still help the team."

"No, I think I'll leave that alone. Besides, I need to help Dad tonight. We're going to get ready for a fishing trip down south this weekend."

"Sounds like fun. Maybe we could go together some time—like old times."

"Suits me! I'll bet our dads would enjoy it too."

The young men began walking their separate ways.

"Oh, A. J.! Remember, 'softer than velvet!'"

A. J. turned back and flashed a wide grin of approval. Then, with a gesture of victory, he responded, "and stronger than steel!"

CPSIA information can be obtained at www.ICGtesting.com
Printed in the USA
LVOW07s2330091213

364534LV00002B/2/P